James Thomson

Northumbria - The Captive Chief

And Other Poems

NORTHUMBRIA

THE CAPTIVE CHIEF

AND OTHER POEMS

BY

JAMES THOMSON

Third Edition—Enlarged

ALNWICK: H. H. BLAIR

1881

James Thomson

Northumbria - The Captive Chief
And Other Poems

ISBN/EAN: 9783337158255

Printed in Europe, USA, Canada, Australia, Japan

Cover: Foto ©Andreas Hilbeck / pixelio.de

More available books at **www.hansebooks.com**

DEDICATED

BY PERMISSION

TO

LADY FAIRFAX.

———

HAVING SERVED YOUR LADYSHIP'S FATHER AND GRANDFATHER

IN THE CAPACITY OF A SERVANT

THE AUTHOR FEELS THAT HE IS PLACING

This Little Volume

UNDER THE PROTECTION OF ONE WHO TAKES AN

INTEREST IN ITS SUCCESS.

PREFACE TO THE THIRD EDITION.

———o———

In the preface to the first edition of my little volume,
I said that " poems by a working man had ceased to
be a novelty." If this was the case ten years ago, it
may be safely affirmed that the number of versifiers
like myself have increased during that time twenty-
fold. The motives that lead many to try their hand at
verse-making are no doubt as varied as the individuals
themselves.

When I first tried my own hand at versifying, I
had no thought of ever making a book ; that was an
after-thought, prompted by a desire to gather together
all my stray pieces : in doing this I found that several
of them had been lost. I was not requested and pressed
by friends and advisers to *print ;* but when I did so,
nothing gave me greater pleasure and satisfaction than

the kindly criticisms passed upon my little volume. I trust that the same kind indulgence will be extended to this, my third and enlarged edition, which I now place in the hands of my friends and the public.

JAMES THOMSON.

SHAWDON, *June* 1, 1881.

PREFACE TO THE FIRST EDITION.

—o—

"Poems by a working man" have ceased to be a
novelty. A professor of the divine art of poesy, at a
public meeting some years ago, gave the world a rough
estimate of the number of imitators of the heaven-born
art in Great Britain. The number was so astounding
that I felt a sort of guilty criminality for ever having
scribbled verses. Under this feeling I am constrained
to make all due apology to those that have the spirit,
and "are sent to prophesy." To the public I offer
no apology; for do not they in great numbers buy
plated goods, and vile prints that would shock the
taste of "*cultivated minds*"? To the small portion
of the public which includes my personal friends and
acquaintances, I give my best thanks for their confi-
dence and generosity in so liberally subscribing towards
my little book before they saw its size or contents. If
they find any pleasure in its perusal, I shall feel a

satisfaction that is perhaps only felt by those that make a book.

> " Some rhyme a neighbour's name to lash,
> Some rhyme, vain thought, for needful cash,
> Some rhyme to raise the country clash."

The last-named motive is perhaps the most potent with rhymers like myself—and why not? The most illiterate may have a yearning after that immortality that is only granted to "the gods;" for have we not eyes? have we not ears? and have we not a heart that can feel and love, although it cannot express its emotions in language measured by the rules of art? Are such to hold their tongues, "even from good words"?

An old bookmaker has said, "What your hand findeth to do, do it with diligence." Acting upon this precept, I launch my little volume upon the ocean, to sink or swim.

JAMES THOMSON.

SHAWDON, *July* 28, 1871.

CONTENTS.

-o——

NORTHUMBRIA:

A POEM.

" Northumberland, I scarce can tell
   Why all thy scenes I love so well ;
   For in thy limits every hill,
   Each lonely cairn and rushing rill,
   Each sheltered strip of stunted wood,
   Thy quiet nooks of solitude,
   Thy liquid fountains gushing clear,
   All on my memory linger dear.
   Nor less do I delight to trace,
   On hill and dale, each noted place
   Connected with a former age,
   That glows upon thy storied page."
                         —ROBERT WHITE.

NORTHUMBRIA:

A POEM.

—o—

NORTHUMBRIA, be thou my theme ;
Thy hills, thy vales, and every stream
That winds through rocky glens their way,
Where busy mankind seldom stray.
There sweet Nature loves to dwell
And bloom unseen in many a dell,
'Mid rocks, and boulders piled on high
In Gothic grandeur to the sky ;
There russet moss and lichens rare
Their colours blend in tints as fair
As the bright rainbow in the sky,
That spans the Cheviot tops on high.
The wild thyme hangs in festoons there,
Its perfume scents the mountain air,
Wafted on the balmy breeze ;
It brings from far the toiling bees ;

From flower to flower on tireless wing,
They sip its sweets, and joyous sing.
The harebell, tinted like the sky,
Waves o'er yon beetling cliff on high,
There the starling takes her rest,
And the martin builds her nest.
And when the evening shadows close,
The cuckoo there takes short repose ;
Ready at dawn to trim her wing,
And hail anew the joyous spring ;
Swift skimming through the ferny dell,
She wakes up Echo in his cell.
Her ringing wild notes, rich and clear,
The wandering shepherd stops to hear ;
It tells him that the time is near—
To every shepherd's heart so dear—
When he shall see his lambkins play
Around their dams, on hill and brae.
Stretched on the grass beside them there,
He'll soon forget his toils and care,
And note with joy around him rise,
And spread their beauty to the skies,
Day by day he sees unrolled,
The tender ferns, bronzed like gold.
Thus Nature springs at God's command,
And clothes anew a barren land.
Stirred by the breath of genial spring,
These barren hills rejoice and sing ;

The tender grass beneath our feet
Is gemmed with many a wild flower sweet.
Thus Nature's ever-bounteous hand
Opens wide at His command :
That mountain ash stood leafless there,
With blossoms now it scents the air ;
And that tall foxglove on the rock
At Nature's call to life awoke,
And like a pennon waves on high
Its flower-clad banner to the sky.
By mountain streams, that ceaseless flow,
The graceful lady-ferns grow,
There weeping birch and alders green
Spread o'er their heads a leafy screen ;
Here in many a sylvan spot,
There blooms the sweet forget-me-not ;
Like some dear memory fed by love,
It takes its hue from heaven above,
And blooms unseen to mortal eye,
But blooms, alas ! to fade and die.
Thus cruel death at last destroys
Our brightest hopes, our loves and joys ;
No vernal sun, nor spring, nor rain,
Will stir them into life again.
How sweet amidst these hills to stray
And spend the lengthened summer day,
Far from the tumult and the strife,
The ceaseless din of city life ;

No discord here, no jarring sound
To break the peaceful calm around.
The murmuring stream, the rushing rill
That leaps in cascades down the hill,
In fitful music breaks the calm,
That rise and falls like some sweet psalm
That soothes to rest the weary heart,
That makes the tear unconscious start.
Amidst such scenes we feel a peace
That to these lonely hills we trace.
Upon that wide expanding waste
A death-like silence seems to rest ;
The cloud that crowns yon towering hill
Is resting there so calm and still ;
Though distant far, it seems so near
That we expect a voice to hear—
The same as when the Almighty spoke
To men from Sinai's towering rock,
And rolling thunders rent the sky,
And Israel felt that God was nigh.

While through these rugged hills I climb,
My thoughts dwell on a bygone time,
When the polecat, wolf, and fox
Lived undisturbed amidst these rocks,
In ancient times here lived a race,
Whose footsteps in these wilds we trace.

Beneath yon cairn piled on high,
The bones of some great chieftain lie,
Who spent his rude and barbarous life
Amidst wild scenes of savage strife.
That pathway leading through the glen
Was trodden by a race of men,
Who sallied forth at dawn of day
To seek their food like beasts of prey ;
These savage men in ambush lay
Where Coquet winds his devious way,
There they watched the milk-white steer
Descend to drink the water clear.
Unconscious that his foes are nigh,
He drinks, and rears his head on high :
Then quick he sniffs the tainted air
That tells his deadly foes are there ;
Then thick as hailstones from the sky
Their spears and arrows round him fly :
Soon vanquished in the unequal strife,
The noble beast yields up his life,
Falls like a heap of driven snow
That winter winds together blow.
Quick from his limbs the skin they tear,
And home the flesh in triumph bear
To their dark den and dwelling-place,
Whose rude foundation here we trace,*

* On Greenshaw Hill, between Linnop and Hartside, the foun-

Where the morning meal is spread,
And there the wretched inmates fed
On sodden flesh torn from the bone
With their rude knives of flinty stone;
There, hidden from the light of day,
These savage men devoured their prey.
The naked children crawling round;
Mix with the dogs upon the ground,
With greedy eyes the fire they watch,
And from its embers quickly snatch
The broiling flesh from off the bone,
Then fly with it to be alone,
Like some greedy beast of prey
That hates to feed in open day.
Thus lived our Pictish sires of old
In misery, nakedness, and cold;
In holes and dens, like beast of prey,
They spent their lives from day to day;
In mental darkness black as night,
Their souls without one ray of light;

---

dations of British towns can be distinctly traced; and a road
or trackway, the work of the same people, leads from the prin-
cipal town down to the Breamish, and on to the hills beyond,
towards the head of the Coquet. There can be little doubt but
that along this track the savage people carried home the wild
animals killed in the forests around the base of the Cheviots;
and there can be as little doubt that amongst them were the
predecessors of the now celebrated wild cattle of Chillingham.

The starry heavens above their head,
They looked upon with fear and dread.
When meteors crossed the midnight sky,
In terror to their gods they cry,
To shield them from the demon's ire
That feeds in heaven the quenchless fire,
Whose flickering flame is seen to play
In the far north at close of day ;
He who, when his anger burns,
The light of day to darkness turns ;
Comes thundering forth in cloudy car,
Its rolling wheels are heard afar ;
The trembling earth beneath them shakes,
And birds and beasts in terror quake.
Like flaming arrows through the sky,
His dreadful lightnings quickly fly ;
They strike and rend the solid rock,
And tare to shreds the mighty oak,
And lay its spreading branches low,
Clothed with the sacred mistletoe.
Struck by a fiery bolt from heaven,
Their sacred oak is rent and riven ;
At the dread sight they prostrate fall,
And to their gods in terror call.
They call in vain, no god draws near,
With helping hand, nor voice to cheer.
At length a human voice they hear,
A man in sable garb draws near ;

With hands uplifted to the sky,
He fervent prayed to God on high
That he, a sinful man and weak,
Might wisely to the people speak
Words of wisdom, power, and might,
Blessed by the Spirit's heavenly light.
Thus prayed Paulinus, while he stood
Surrounded by the heathen crowd.
Then aloud he cried : "Draw near,
All ye that sit in darkness hear :
To me, O people, words are given
To tell you from the God of heaven,
Who sent His Son from heaven above.
To tell men of His matchless love.
The gods you worship are no gods at all,
They cannot see you prostrate fall ;
They have no ears, nor eyes to see
You worship 'neath that spreading tree ;
But God, with His all-seeing eye,
Sees you kneel, and hears you cry.
To Him, O sinful people, pray
That He may wash your sins away,
And ere your wretched lives are done
Reveal to you His blessed Son.
All you that now before Him stand,
Are made and fashioned by His hand ;
He made the sun so dazzling bright,
And you rejoice to see His light.

The moon and stars He likewise made,
That sparkle nightly o'er your head.
Look to yonder distant shore,
Where foaming billows toss and roar :
God made the sea, at His command
Its waves break harmless on the sand.
He made the beasts, and birds of air,
The spreading trees, and flowers so fair ;
He sends the snow and summer rain,
And clothes these hills in green again.
Though we His presence cannot see,
Yet He is near to you and me.
To me, O people, the mission's given
To tell you of the God of heaven,
Whose blessèd Son came from above
To tell men of their Father's love ;
He came the Saviour of men to be,
And lived and died for you and me :
He wandered far o'er hill and glen,
To preach and speak to sinful men ;
The words He said I now tell you,
If you believe you'll find them true."
While on a rock Paulinus stood,*
He lifted high the holy rood

—

* Paulinus, the first missionary to the pagan Northumbrians,
whose name is associated with many of the streams and holy

(The cross-bar was taken from the tree
Whereon Christ died in agony);
The upright shaft of polished oak
He planted firmly on the rock.
The people saw with wondering eyes
The first cross in Northumbria rise,
And flocked in crowds from far and near
The story of the cross to hear.
As Christ's forerunner did of old,
The sainted man the story told—
How Christ, the blessèd Lamb of God,
In human form the earth He trode.
"Look to that cross!" Paulinus cried;
"Thereon your Saviour bled and died;
Now on a throne He sits in heaven,
And unto Him all power is given."
It was thus Paulinus did unfold,
And to crowds the story told;
O'er many a wild and rugged way
He wandered far, to preach and pray.
Through danger, misery, and strife
He held aloft the lamp of life—

wells in the North, was obliged, A.D. 633, to leave the country.
After the death of Edwin, slain in the battle of Hatfield, near
Doncaster, he took with him into Kent the widow and children
of the fallen king. There he ended his long and useful life as
Bishop of Rochester.

The lamp divine, the heavenly light,
That chase away the shades of night.
Quenched quickly like a beacon fire,
He saw the heavenly light expire.
With Edwin slain on Hatfield moor,
Northumbria saw its darkest hour.
From the Trent to winding Forth
The heathen triumphed o'er the North;
Blood and rapine raged around,
The Cross of Christ cast to the ground,
The powers of evil ruled once more,
" The Man of God" fled from the shore.
In distant Kent he ne'er ceased to pray
For loved Northumbria far away,
That God would quell the heathen's rage
And give Christ back His heritage.

It was in his country's darkest hour
That Oswald came, in might and power;
Oswald—no more glorious name
In dark Northumbrian history gleam.*

---

* After the death of Edwin the people relapsed into idolatry again,
until Oswald, another of Ethelfrith's sons, slew the murderous
Cadwalla, at Heventield, near Hexham. Amongst his first acts
was to send to Iona for a bishop to restore the Christian religion
in the land. There he had himself, when in exile, received a

Like the shining star so bright,
That ushers in the morning light,
His heart aglow with holy fire,
To mighty deeds he did aspire.
On Hevenfield that glorious day,
Pierced by his spear, Cadwalla lay.
For this glorious victory given,
He knelt before the God of heaven,
And vowed, if he was granted life,
To put an end to war and strife—
Raise up the fallen cross again,
That trampled in the dust had lain.
To aid his holy work the while,
There came from lone Iona's isle
Aidan, that Christ-like man—
The holy work again began.
Like the beloved John of old,
In loving words he did unfold
The mystery of redeeming love,
Vouchsafed to man from heaven above.

---

knowledge of the Christian faith. The authorities of that place
sent him an austere man, Corman by name, who failed in his
mission. On his return to Iona, Aidan remarked: "Brother,
by thy own showing thou hast gone the wrong way to work;
thou hast given the children strong meat instead of milk."
Aidan appeared the right man for the great work, and he will-
ingly left his quiet life in Iona for the troubled career of a
Northumbrian bishop.

The people wondered, and adored,
And bent the knee before the Lord.
The image of the mighty Thor
They burned upon the sandy shore,
Cast Woden's temples to the ground,
And strewed the sacred fire around.
No more to him they bent the knee,
In terror, 'neath the sacred tree ;
To God beneath the azure skies
They offered prayer, as sacrifice.
The sainted Aidan, worn with toil,
Turned his thoughts to Farne Isle ;
He longed to build a temple there,
And end his life in fast and prayer.
No temple yet was seen to rise
Beneath Northumbria's wide-spread skies ;
No holy altar to the Lord,
Where His name might be adored.
Like the Israelites of old,
A willing people gave their gold ;
The poorest did an offering bring,
And laid it down before the king.
Oswald took their offering meet,
And laid it at Aidan's feet,
Therewith to build unto the Lord
A house, where He might be adored.
Then quickly at the king's command
Messengers went through the land,

To tell the people all to pray
Upon the great Ascension Day;
For on that day, on Farne Isle,
They meant to found a holy pile.

That morning rose, bright and fair,
A balmy fragrance filled the air;
The dew o'er all the landscape lay,
And sparkled in the sunny ray.
On Cheviot-top a fleecy cloud
Lay glittering, like a silver shroud;
Peace seemed brooding o'er the deep,
The troubled waves were hushed in sleep:
The noisy sea-birds ceased to scream,
And on its bosom seemed to dream.
From the green earth there did arise
A fragrant incense to the skies;
From every vale and upland glen
Went, seaward, troops of savage men;
All their thoughts are turned the while,
To meet their king on Farne Isle.
King Oswald at the dawn of day
Left Bamborough castle grey;
He bade his boatmen, with a smile,
Row him hence to Farne Isle.
The people saw their king draw near,
And hailed him with a lusty cheer;
As soon as he had touched the land,
Aidan took him by the hand,

And led him through the motley crowd;
The while a psalm he chanted loud,
Until he reached the chosen ground,
With all the chiefs assembled round.
The holy stone, prepared with care,
Suspended hung already there.
The king a silver trowel took,
Then raised to heaven a silent look:
On bended knees, with arms bare,
He laid the corner-stone with care;
Then with his spear he struck the ground,
And spoke to those assembled round:
" You, my loving people, witness be
This day between the Lord and me,
That I to God this island give,
That here His saints may ever live,
And ever in His presence stand,
And pray for this belovèd land."
" O God of heaven," Aidan said,
" This holy work vouchsafe to aid;
May here until time's latest day,
Thy servants never cease to pray.
We take in trust this gift for heaven,
By thee, O king, so freely given;
And at this shrine, by night and day,
For thee, O king, we'll ever pray."

God on the holy work did smile,
And quickly rose the sacred pile—

So quickly, that the people said
That unseen hands had given aid
To carve and shape so quaint and fair
That arch suspended in the air ;
The massive columns, cut in stone,
Must be the work of gods alone.
Above the arch-encircled door
A richly-carvèd figure bore
A polished cross of marble stone,
That brightly like a mirror shone.
To see this house so fair and meet,
Pilgrims came with weary feet ;
The rudest felt an holy awe
When this glorious shrine they saw ;
With feet unshod they entered there,
And knelt to God in heartfelt prayer,
And sought within this holy place
The pardon of their sins, and grace.
There the holy Aidan vigils kept—
Prayed to God while others slept,
That He would vengeance quickly bring
Upon the slayers of his king.
Within these walls St. Cuthbert prayed,*
And here his holy bones were laid,

---

* The name of St. Cuthbert is so identified with the early
history of the Christian Church of Northumberland that every

Exempt, it is said, from that decay
That turns the mortal frame to clay.

Alas! thy glories now are gone,
Time's fingers waste thy carvèd stone;
Instead of solemn chant and prayer,
The rude winds sing a requiem there.
Long may thy mouldering ruins stand,
Safe from the spoiler's ruthless hand.

---

schoolboy ought to know how much they owe to the great and
good men who first taught the heathen people of Northumbria
the Gospel of Christ. Although much that is legendary is
interwoven with the history of St. Cuthbert, enough remains
to testify that he was no ordinary man. The Venerable Bede
tells us that from his very childhood he was inflamed with the
desire to devote his life to the glory of God. He heard with the
deepest sorrow that he had been unanimously elected to be a
bishop. He would have rather spent the last days of his life
in solitude and prayer. There is no more interesting episode
in the whole history of the early Church in Britain than the
disinterring of the body of St. Cuthbert by the Bishop and
monks of Lindisfarne, and flying with it from place to place,
to escape the bloody Danes who had pillaged the country.
Bede informs us that the saint's body was found "like one
asleep; even the vestments of the body were fresh, and had
their gloss upon them." There is little doubt but that many
of the early churches in Northumberland were built upon spots
where the sacred body of St. Cuthbert rested. Along with his
body they carried the mangled head of St. Oswald, who fell in
battle, A.D. 642, fighting against the pagan king Penda, the last
pagan king of the North, who was drowned in a swollen river
near Leeds.

'Tis not for me in rustic verse
Thy by-past glories to rehearse ;
The ruin that upon thee fell,
The mournful page of history tell :
With musing thoughts I turn the while,
And, lingering, leave the Holy Isle.

THE CAPTIVE CHIEF:

A TALE OF FLODDEN FIELD.

BEHIND the Cheviots sank the sun
Ere Flodden's fatal fight was done,
And night's dark curtain gently fell *
On such a scene as none can tell.
Scotland's brave host that morn arose
Burning to meet their Southern foes ;—
Ere eve, beside meand'ring Till,
That warlike host in death lay still :
Like autumn leaves cast to the ground,
There lay the dead and dying round,
Thick as the grain from sower's hand
Lies scattered o'er the furrowed land :

---

* This memorable battle, so disastrous to Scotland, was fought
on the 9th of September 1513. It began about four o'clock in
the afternoon, and continued until darkness covered the scene.
The gallant King of Scotland, James IV., was slain, with two
bishops, four abbots, twelve earls, seventeen lords, four hundred
knights ; and from ten to twelve thousand of the Scottish host
were left lifeless upon " Flodden's fatal field."

So lay proud Scotland's warriors brave,
None left to dig a brother's grave.
Oh, fatal field!—oh, mournful day!
When prince and peasant lifeless lay.
Fenced round with bodies of the dead,
Their king lies there, with crownless head.
Brave as the lion on his shield,
He thought to turn the wavering field;
But, ah, alas! 'twas all in vain,
He dealt his blows with strength amain;
First in the fight he scorned to fly—
"Death, or victory!" was his cry.

The dawning morn revealed to view
His mangled body wet with dew;*
Stripped by the spoiler's ruthless hand,
There lay the King of fair Scotland,

---

* The dead body of the king was discovered amidst a heap of slain, despoiled and stripped of his armour, and covered with ghastly wounds. For twenty-five years he had worn an iron chain round his loins in penance for having appeared at the head of the rebels who killed his father, James III., against his express orders. To this chain he added a link every year in testimony of his deep sorrow. All history speaks of King James IV. as brave and generous to an extreme, majestic in countenance, with the wonderful art of winning all hearts to his person and cause. He was killed in the twenty-fifth year of his reign, and the thirty-ninth of his age.

Nought left to tell his princely state,
To mark him out as high and great,—
Nought, save the chain he meekly wore
Around his loins in penance sore.

The Tindale thieves, like birds of prey,*
Hung round the field and watched the fray.
Wild Branxton, with the bloody hand,
Led on that fierce and lawless band :
Each with a pine-torch flaming bright
Rushed forth like demons of the night
To crown the horrors of that day,
And spoil the fallen where they lay.
They stripped the dead and wounded bare
Of all they wore was rich or rare.

One noble youth, whose fine array
Bespoke the warrior rich and gay,
Lay with his wounded bosom bare,
That showed a jewelled cross hung there.

---

* When darkness had spread its pall over this field of the
dead, the thieves of Tindale and Teviotdale fell upon the dead
and dying like birds of prey, and stripped them of their armour
and everything valuable about their persons. The king and
his nobles were amongst the first to undergo this degradation,
the thieves selecting those first who wore the richest housings.
It would be impossible to portray by pen or pencil the scene
that presented itself to the eyes of those who saw the " fatal
field " on the morning after this memorable and bloody battle.

Calm as a sleeping child he lay,
But then anon was heard to pray:
"God save our country; shield our king,
Spread o'er his head Thy sheltering wing.
For him we'll spend our blood and breath,
On—on to victory or to death!"
His broken spear he reared on high,
And shouted loud his gathering cry;
Quick o'er his frame a shudder passed,
The broken spear fell from his grasp.

Branxton the scene in silence eyed.
"Faddon, help here!" he sharply cried.
A mounted horn that loosely hung
Quick from his belt the chief unslung,
Then loosed the dying warrior's casque,
And pressed to's lips the gen'rous flask.
He felt the wine his strength renew,
A laboured breath at length he drew,
And gazed on chief in mute surprise,
As one that doth from trance arise.
Then quick and soft the warrior spoke,
His voice in Celtic accents broke:
"Tell me if ye be friend or foe?
Have we the vict'ry?—ay or no?
No!—Is our king safe, or is he slain?
Slain!—Then, O God! all hope is vain.

Oh! welcome death! I long to die,
And be with those that round me lie.
My country! oh, I weep for thee!
My mountain home no more I'll see!
But home's not home if slaves we be;
Then welcome death and grave to me."
A sigh of sorrow heaved his breast,
And to his heart the cross he prest.

Upon crossed spears they placed a shield,
And bore the chieftain from the field
To where the stolen horses stood,
And placed him on a litter rude;
A martial cloak they round him threw,
To shield him from the midnight dew.
Laden with spoil, the Bloody Hand
Drew from the field his savage band;
By Langleyford they took their way,
Long ere the Cheviots smiled in day.
They halted at the noontide hour
Where Linhope's waters downward pour.
Loud was the noise, and wild the din,
That echoed in the rocky linn:
Drunk with the spoil of others' woe,
The ribald song and wine did flow;
The beacon blazed on Simond's height
Long ere they halted for the night.

At last they reached lone Coquet-side ;
There for the night they meant to bide.
Their watch-fire cast its lurid gleam
On tangled brake and winding stream ;
The night-birds rose in wild dismay,
And, screaming, took their flight away.

Worn with the toils of night and day,
Soon on the earth each dalesman lay ;
Some 'mong the brackens made their bed,
Some sought the pine-tree's darker shade.
Their captive lay as in a dream
Still-listening to the warbling stream.
At last he slept in calm repose,
Oblivious of his wounds and woes,
Till startled by a bugle sound
That echoed from the rocks around.
At that sharp sound each dalesman rose,
All prompt to meet their chasing foes.
The blast was but the warder's call
That paced Harbottle's dark-grey wall.*

---

* Harbottle Castle, now in ruins, stands on a commanding
eminence above the river Coquet. We read that it was given
by William the Conqueror, in the tenth year of his reign, to
Robert de Umfranville, Knight, Lord of Tours and Vian, to keep
and to hold, by defending that part of the country for ever from
enemies and wolves, with the sword which the said King Wil-

But quick they mustered man and beast,
And left the place in speedy haste;
The captive chief they left behind,
Like some lost garment out of mind.
Unconscious of their flight he lay
Till dawn had brightened into day;
Then round the scene a look he cast,
And wished that it might be his last.
He thought of his dear Highland home,
Where, as a boy, he used to roam,
Dreaming of war and high renown;—
But all those airy dreams have flown.

The Rose of Coquet chanced to stray
Past where the wounded chieftain lay;

---

liam had by his side when he entered Northumberland. In the
reign of King Henry II. this castle was taken by the Scots, but
was soon recovered again. It was used as a stronghold or prison
for all depredators taken within the Middle Marches.

It was also in this castle that the widowed Queen of James
IV. (killed at Flodden), about a year after this event, married
Archibald Douglas, Earl of Angus, by whom she had a beautiful
daughter, Margaret, born in 1516 at Harbottle Castle, afterwards
married to Matthew Stuart, Earl of Lennox, mother to Henry
Lord Darnley, husband of Mary Queen of Scots, and father of
James VI., first King of England and Scotland.

The scenery in the neighbourhood of Harbottle and Holystone
is lovely and romantic, and has many features in common with
the Highland scenery of Scotland.

Warder, her fleet and noble hound,
Sprang on the chief with savage bound.
"Down, Warder, down!" the maiden cried,
And quick her order was obeyed.
"Whom have we here?" she softly said,
While rising blush her face o'erspread.
The chieftain met her wondering gaze
Dumb with surprise and strange amaze;
He thought some angel from the skies
Looked down on him with pitying eyes.
A golden fillet bound her hair,
That reached her waist in tresses fair;
Her eyes appeared of liquid blue,
And sparkled like the morning dew;
Her ungloved hand, so small and fair,
Held in its grasp a volume rare;
She stood in all her queenly grace,
Fair as the Naiad of the place.
The chieftain told his mournful tale,
And saw a tear unconscious steal
From her sweet eyes; it seemed to flow
In pity at his tale of woe.

"You are my captive *now*," she said,
"And in my dungeon must be laid."
Straight back to castle then she went,
And six strong yeomen quickly sent
To bring the chief, with speed and care,

To the west tower, and place him there,
Upon Earl Gilbert's damask bed,
Where that great warrior's spirit fled.
From autumn till sweet flowery May
The chief in that lone chamber lay.
Many a dull and dreary hour
He spent in that great western tower,
Nought save the convent's tolling bell
To break the silence of the dell.
But oft at eve a sound more sweet
His longing heart and ears would greet,
A sound that made his heart to glow
With a sweet joy that few can know.
A maiden struck the trembling string
Of her sweet harp, and then would sing
A song of sorrow and of woe,
That made the tears unconscious flow—
A song of love and lover lost,
Ta'en captive by the Sar'cen host;
Then she would strike a martial strain,
Such as we ne'er shall hear again,
Of battle's din and wild turmoil,
That made the blood to dance and boil.
The wounded chief longed for the hour
And strength to leave his prison-tower.

Restored at last, he sought the hall,
And for his captor fair did call.

She came with all her wonted grace,
A smile lit up her beaming face;
But when she caught the chieftain's eyes
A mantling blush began to rise.
The chief bowed low, then, faltering, said:
" I come to thank you, gen'rous maid;
Your slave and servant I must be,
My life, my all, I owe to thee."
" My captive, then, I set you free
From all allegiance due to me;
You're free from this, at any hour,
To leave Harbottle's ancient tower.
Go to your home and clansmen brave,
Where the brown heath and tartans wave,
And seek no more our Border strife,
Where men so cheaply sell their life."

But ere he left the Coquet-side,
Its fairest flower bloomed as his bride;
He wed fair Ros'mond with that ring,
The gift of his beloved king;
And long she lived to bless the day
That she by Coquet-side did stray,
And found a wounded chieftain there,—
Her husband long,—the great St. Clair.

AUTUMN LEAVES.

In early spring we love to see
The budding leaves on hedge and tree,
As day by day before our eyes
They spread their beauty to the skies ;
Fair as when the Almighty spoke,
And trees and flowers to life awoke ;
The beauteous earth, like some fair queen,
That day appeared all clothed in green.

As each successive season flies,
New wonders pass before our eyes ;
The woodlands, once so bright and green,
Now hastening to decay are seen.
O'er corn-fields and leafy glade
Sere autumn's mantle now is spread,
A varied landscape lies unrolled
Harmonious mixed, with green and gold.

As through the woods I musing stray,
The falling leaves bestrew my way—

Tossed by September's fitful blast,
Like spray of ocean landward cast,
Upon a wild and trackless shore,
To vanish, and be seen no more ;
The summer leaves once bright and green
Drop earthward, and are no more seen.

Short and changeful as an autumn day,
Like leaves of summer men decay ;
In life's bright spring his heart is light,
Hope cheers him on with visions bright,
Happy if in life's swift advancing years
A cloudless sun his pathway cheers,
Lighting him onward to a changeless clime
Unmeasured by the lapse of time.

AUTUMN BERRIES.

Autumn berries all aglow,
Some like gold and some like snow,
Some like diamonds brightly shine,
Some like rubies in the mine.
Where the gossamer loves to play,
And stretch his threads across the way.
There bright rosy hips are seen,
Hawberries shining out between.

There, trailing low upon the ground,
Brambleberries black are found ;
Bright as coal dug from the seam,
In the autumn sun they gleam.
Here the schoolboy loves to stray,
When home at eve he wends his way ;
Nature for him spreads here a feast
That pampered children never taste.

In after-years will memory turn
To some such spot beside the burn,

Where with companions free and wild
We roamed 'mid Nature, Nature's child,
Free as the scented autumn breeze
That shook the acorns from the trees,
Strewed the ground with yellow leaves
That smelt as sweet as harvest sheaves.

Then home we bore, with joy and glee,
The rich wild fruit from bush and tree ;
Crabs and nuts, with jet-black sloes,
Hips shining brighter than the rose.
Snowberries whiter than the snow,
Around our caps in wreaths did glow ;
We made the woodlands ring with joy,
That told our hearts had no alloy.

THE FISHERMAN'S WIFE.

" RAISE me higher, mother dear,
　　And open wide the door,
That I may see his boat come in
　　And land upon the shore.
' Nell, my lass,' he said to me
　　When first he brought me hame,
' The new boat that's to win our bread,
　　Must bear your ain sweet name.

" ' To-morrow you must christen her,
　　Before she gans to sea—
The boat that bears my Nelly's name
　　Will bring great luck to me.'
But now, alas ! I canna gang
　　To push her from the shore,
Nor help my man to land his boat,
　　As oft I've done before.

" But raise me higher, mother dear,
　　And prop my weary head ;

Let my last look be on the sea
   Where Aleck wins his bread.
God guard my honest fisherman
   Upon the mighty deep;
There hard he toils to win his bread,
   While thousands soundly sleep.

" My sight is growing dim, mother,
   I canna see the shore ;
But I can hear it's Aleck's foot
   That now comes to the door.
Take my hand in yours, Aleck,
   And speak my name once more,
Just as you used to whisper it
   When we walked on the shore.

" When I am dead and gone, Aleck,
   You'll sometimes think of me,
As you toil through the weary night
   Upon the stormy sea.
God bring you aye safe to the shore,
   And keep you till you die ;
Then, Aleck dear, we'll meet again
   In a home beyon' the sky."

When Aleck's boat is far at sea,
   And the stars shine o'er his head,

He looks up to them longingly,
    And thinks of her that's dead ;
When the waves are tossed by angry winds,
    And the loud tempests roar,
Then Aleck's heart longs for that rest
    Where Helen's gone before.

LINES TO A CHILD ON HER FIRST BIRTHDAY.

DEAR child, on this your natal day
In heartfelt words for you I pray,
That each succeeding year you see
May happier than the bygone be.
When infant years are passed away,
And you in happy girlhood play,
Gathering daisies sweet and fair,
To wreathe them in your flowing hair,
May your heart, like that sweet flower,
Expand and bloom in sunny bower,
Sheltered from the storms and strife
That spoil our joys and cloud our life.
When you reach your maiden prime,
And taste the bliss of that sweet time,
May you from heaven direction seek,
For in our strength we are but weak.
From all the snares that round you lie,
God guard you with His watchful eye—
Give you true wisdom from above,
And fill your heart with heavenly love.

If heaven grant you e'er to know
The sweetest bliss of earth below,—
Domestic joys, with that maternal love,
That have their source in heaven above
(These, like tender, fragile flowers,
That only bloom in sunny bowers),—
Be it yours to tend with loving care
Those tender flowers, so sweet and fair;
That they may shed their sweet perfume
Like gathered roses in a room.
As summer follows after spring,
And autumn golden treasures bring,
May each successive season bring to you
Heavenly blessings, like the dew;
That, when the final call is given,
It finds you ripe, and meet for heaven.

LINES TO A CAGED LARK.

MINSTREL of early spring, bird of the skies !
With feelings sad I hear your song arise ;
In this dark, wretched alley, named a street,
Your heaven-tuned notes rise high and sweet ;
Even here kind Nature stirs within your breast
A song of joy that cannot be repressed,—
Caged like a felon, yet you murmur not,
Nor pine in sorrow at your hapless lot.

Sweet bird, I long to set you free,
That you might spread your wings and flee
To meadows green, where early daisies spring
And birds fly free on lightsome wing.
Caged in this noisome alley, dark and drear,
Your song perchance some weary heart may cheer—
Some longing heart that ne'er again will see
The daisied sward nor leaf-clad tree.

Dear bird, it stirs my heart to hear
Your song in sweet notes trilling clear,

High o'er the ceaseless turmoil and the din,
The seething flood of strife and sin.
Amongst the surging crowd that floats along,
Some pause and listen to your song;
And as they listen, memories sweet arise,
Of country scenes and cloudless skies.

In yonder wretched garret there is laid
The wreck of what was once a maid;
She tries, alas! but tries in vain, to pray;
Her thoughts are wandering far away—
Amongst green fields, where cowslips spring,
Where oft she heard the sweet lark sing;
She lifts her weary head to hear again
Your matchless song, a heaven-taught strain.

It wafts her thoughts back to that home
Where she in youth was wont to roam;
There, beneath the apple-blossomed tree,
She strung bright cowslips from the lea.
Pure as the white flower on the thorn,
She trod the dew at early morn;
And like that flower plucked from the spray,
As soon as faded cast away.

THE CHRISTMAS ROSE.

PALE flower, thou hang'st thy drooping head
Like a lone widow mourning o'er the dead ;
Bereft of all the sweet and lovely flowers,
That deck gay summer's leafy bowers :
The fallen leaves of autumn round thee lie,
To rot beneath chill winter's leaden sky ;
You bloom alone, a solitary flower,
And know no summer sun nor shower.
In dark and evil days your lot is cast,
Unsheltered you must bear the blast ;
Like some lone spirit in life's darkened hour,
You bend beneath the blast, sweet tender flower :
Men heedless pass you in their way,
And at thy shrine no rapturous homage pay,
But kneel to some frail and fleeting flower
That blooms and dies within an hour,
And needs the sun's bright shining ray
To paint their transient colours gay :
To them the poet tunes his sweetest lays,
And rapturous crowds prolong their praise.

Sweet, lonely flower, you're ever dear to me,
In thy pale bloom I more than beauty see—
A type, an emblem of the Child that lay
Cradled in a manger on this blessed day.
Neglected by the crowd that throngs around,
But by the heaven-directed found ;
That like the shepherds come to pay
Their heartfelt homage on thy natal day,
And like the wise men from the East,
Who at Thy feet their offerings placed,
They humbly give thee praise and prayer,
Their heart's best gifts they offer there.
Emblem of Him, sweet humble flower,
You come to cheer life's darkest hour.
The rose of Sharon and the lily fair,
With thee, sweet flower, cannot compare ;
Faint emblem thou of the dear Child
That in the manger sweetly smiled,—
No flower more dear to me that blows,
Than thou, pale, lonely Christmas rose.

THE LAST NIGHT O' THE YEAR.

1874.

As I sat musing in the neuk
    The last night o' the year,
My dear, loved wife, wi' busy hands,
    Laid out our New Year's cheer.
When seated round our humble board,
    I briefly said the grace :
As I handed round the cheese and cake,
    My wife looked in my face.

I read the thoughts within her heart,
    Though ne'er a word she spoke ;
The Christmas holly on the walls
    Old memories dear awoke.
Her thoughts were on a New Year's eve,
    Just thirty years ago,—
The first we spent, as man and wife,
    Beside our ingle low.

Since that night time's ruthless hand
    Has changed our yellow hair ;

His finger-prints are on our face,
    That once was smooth and fair.
Though time has changed our outward form,
    Our hearts are still the same ;
There brightly burns love's quenchless fire,
    Not passion's fitful flame.

The setting sun oft clearest shines
    When sinking in the west ;
A halo bright surrounds the spot
    Where he has sunk to rest.
So may it be, my dear, loved wife,
    When our few years are run ;
May we drop peacefully to rest,
    Clear as the setting sun.

These thoughts had passed across my mind,
    When on my ears there fell
A solemn, mournful sound to me,
    The midnight passing bell.
As I listened to its fitful sound,
    Deep thoughts passed through my heart ;
When, lo ! a knock came to the door,
    That made me quickly start.

In haste I ran, unlatched the door,
    And set it to the wa',
When in there stepped the sweetest child
    My eyes yet ever saw ;

A snow-white robe was o'er her thrown,
  Stars sparkled on it bright,
An azure wreath bound up her hair,
  Where shone the Queen of night.

"God hald you hale," I said, "sweet child,
  You are right welcome here;
Be seated by our humble board,
  And taste our New Year's cheer."
When, smiling, she looked in my face,
  I saw her features clear;
I in a moment bent my knee
  Before the infant year.

"Be pleased," I said, "to bless our home
  With peace and sweet content,
And grant us each a thankful heart
  For every blessing sent.
If in your hand you bring the cup
  Of sorrow or of loss,
Let us not grumble at our fate,
  But patient bear our cross.

"And for my country, dear to me,
  I humbly hope you bring
Heaven's choicest blessing in your hand,
  To make us joyful sing

The praise of Him whose mighty hand
    Rules all things here below ;
His power exalteth nations high,
    His nod can lay them low."

TO MR. AND MRS. CLIFF,

ON THEIR GOLDEN WEDDING DAY.

I BEG in humble verse to say,
On this your Golden Wedding day,
That from my heart I wish you joy,
Your peace and hope let nought destroy ;
May your remaining years be blest,
And peaceful as the sea at rest ;
That with calm thought you may survey
The fifty years that have passed away
Since you fulfilled that great command,
In mutual faith joined hand in hand.
Though brief those years may now appear,
To you their memory must be dear,
For heaven has spared you both to see
Three generations smile upon your knee.
In these degenerate days of man,
The longest life is but a span ;
They are few indeed, and far between,
That live to see what you have seen.
Blest with wealth a goodly store,
And like the patriarchs of yore,

You have sons and daughters fair to see,
And goodly as the cedar-tree ;
Sweet buds of promise you have lost,
Nipped by death's untimely frost,
And one fair form, a fruitful tree,
Alas ! no more on earth we'll see.
A loving heart, a cultured mind,
Her motives high, her actions kind ;
By voice and deed she tried to draw
Her kind to study Nature's law ;
To make their homes that pure abode,
And dedicate their lives to God.
Deep in your heart you felt the blow
That all untimely laid her low,
But now your thoughts will often rise
To her bright home beyond the skies.
Friends on earth we love to meet,
Their names are dear, their presence sweet ;
But alas ! as years flow swiftly on,
To-day they are here, to-morrow gone,
But in our hearts their memories dwell,
Deeper far than tongue can tell.
To pen to you on such a happy day,
These lines may seem a cheerless lay.
But life is not a tideless sea,
It has its storms for you and me ;
But when they are past, how clear and bright
The moon breaks through the cloud of night !

Your sorrows I have felt and seen,
And in your joys a sharer I have been,
When round your hearth with joy and glee,
The children hailed the Christmas tree ;
The air rang with their joyous shout,
When round you dealt the golden fruit.
Life to them was bright and fair,
They felt no sorrow, knew no care,
When sheltered in that sacred spot,
Their early home that never is forgot.
Now at that festive time of year,
Their children come your hearts to cheer,
And while they climb upon your knee,
Your early life renewed you see.
To taste such joys long may you live,
The fruits that wedded life can give,   ·
Is the wish and prayer of him who writes
The simple lines that gratitude indites.

WORK, BROTHERS, WORK!

RISE up like men and work and toil,
    The world is a field
That must be tilled before we sow,
    Ere it a harvest yield.
Hold not your hand when dark clouds lower,
    They may quickly pass away ;
If we neglect to sow in spring,
    We'll have no harvest day.

Then rise like men, lay to your hand,
    There is work for all to do ;
If you stand by with folded hands,
    You are no Britons true.
Our country is in danger great,
    But not from foreign foe ;
Vile factions will usurp the state,
    And lay our nation low.

Then be true men, and conquer self,
    No greater work is done
By patriot great, or hero brave,
    Beneath the glorious sun.

When every man this conquest makes,
　　The "good time" is begun,
Then brotherhood and love will reign
　　Till time its course has run.

Rise up like men, strong, brave, and true,
　　Work not for self alone,—
Work for your country and your kind,
　　They'll reap when you are gone.
God worketh on both night and day
　　To carry out His plan—
To make this world a happier place,
　　A paradise for man.

Work, brothers, while it is the day,
　　The night is coming fast,
And when our sun in darkness sets,
　　The time to work is past.
Then we will render up our work
　　Into the Master's hand;
Oh, may it be approved by Him,
　　And in His presence stand!

TUNE THE HARP.

WRITTEN AFTER HEARING MISS KENNEDY SING
"THE FOUR MARIES."

Tune the harp, the sweet-toned harp,
  And softly touch the string;
The melody I loved in youth
  I'll try once more to sing.
Years have fled, and she is gone
  That joined her voice with mine
To sing that song, so sad with woe,
  That stirred our hearts langsyne.

When dark clouds of sorrow hide
  The sunshine from my heart,
The mem'ry of my Mary's form
  Makes tears of sorrow start.
I think upon the happy time,
  Her hand held fast in mine,
We joined our voices in that song
  We loved to sing langsyne.

That melody through years has been
　　Like some sweet dream to me ;
I've heard its music in the breeze
　　That stirs the leafy tree ;
I've heard it in the song of birds,
　　At morning dawn so fair ;
I've heard its sound within my ear,
　　When no voice was there.

To my old heart that melody
　　Comes like the breath of spring ;
It wakens memories in my heart
　　That nothing else will bring.
My native land is rich in song,
　　And sweet old minstrelsy,
But that the song my Mary loved
　　Is dearest still to me.

EPISTLE TO JOHN HICKSON.

THANKS, my friend, for your kind letter,
I've seldom read a sermon better;
You paint our lives in every feature
        With skill and art,
And strike that chord in human nature
        That stirs the heart.

You speak of years now long gone by,
When we were young, and hope was high,
And every object met the eye,
        Tinged like the rose :
All vanished now, we'll let them lie
        In dark repose.

Though they are gone we'll not repine,
There's many a blessing—yours and mine ;
Around our hearth doth brightly shine
        The lamp of love,
Fed by hands we hold divine
        As those above.

From the cold world we gladly turn,
And all its empty pleasures spurn ;
To where the lamp of love doth burn
                    So bright and clear ;
To home our spirits gladly turn,
                    For hope and cheer.

Without a home, to you and me
This world a desert bleak would be,—
A dark and troubled, trackless sea,
                    Without a shore ;
A land where neither flower nor tree
                    Grew round our door.

Upon the hearth we love so dear,
Long may the yule-log burn clear,
With friends around, our hearts to cheer,
                    At Christmas time ;
And laughing plenty ever near
                    To ring the chime.

When round the festive board we sit
With smiling face and harmless wit,
Amidst our mirth we'll not forget
                    The needy poor,
For many foodless, fireless sit
                    At this bright hour.

As years in dark oblivion sink,
It's well, my friend, that we should think
That we draw daily near the brink
            Of death's dark stream,
At thought of which we backward shrink
            As in a dream.

Many a dear, loved friend we mourn,
Has crossed that stream, ne'er to return ;
Their memory in our hearts will burn
            A quenchless fire,
Till we ourselves have crossed that bourn,
            And life expire.

These thoughts, my friend, I send in rhyme,
An offering at this Christmas time ;
Though neither great, nor yet sublime,
            They yet rehearse
My passing thoughts just at this time
            In simple verse.

THE VALE OF WHITTINGHAM.

THE autumn sun had ushered in the day,
And through reft clouds sent forth a ray
That fell on Thrunton's rugged height;
The cold grey rocks sent back the light
Like some faint and waning star
Sinking in the distance far;
No sound is heard from field or hill,
All Nature sleeps in silence still;
The morning is the day of rest
Of all the seven to man the best.
Now silence reigns in forge and hill,
And busy commerce' hand is still;
And toiling man is free to walk abroad,
And hold communion with his God.
Outlined against the morning sky,
The Cheviot Hills around me lie;
Some draped in purple, some in green,
With many a sylvan glade between.
A grey cold mist along the valleys lie,
That hides their beauty from the eye;

When, lo ! the misty vapours grey
Pass like a morning cloud away,—
The sun unclouded, clear and bright,
Fills all these vales with glorious light.
'Mid pastures rich, and meadows green,
Browsing herds may now be seen ;
Where Aln winds its devious way,
The fleecy flocks in thousands stray :
In sweet confusion now are seen
The fields alternate gold and green.
Bright stubble-fields, like maps unrolled,
Shine in the dew like sheets of gold ;
The leaves that clothed the hawthorn spray,
Fall now in showers along the way.
From many a homestead to the skies
The spiral smoke in columns rise—
From hearths where busy hands prepare
The morning meal of homely fare.
But hark ! I hear the joyous knell,
The sweet sound of the Sabbath bell ;
At that sound what memories start,
And sweet emotions fill the heart :
Cold is the heart, and dull that ear,
That all unmoved that sound can hear.
It brings to mind that joyous morn,
When to the church our bride was borne :
It speaketh of a sad and mournful day,
When loved ones in the dust we lay ;

Its tones remind us of a time
When this fair vale was stained with crime—
A time when no sweet Sabbath bell
Upon men's ears like music fell,
Ere yon grey steeple reared its head
Amidst the dwellings of the dead.
But now we hear in every knell
A voice of joy, that seems to tell
That darkness now is passed away,
Like morning mist at dawn of day.

IN MEMORIAM

Of the late Mrs. Davidson, wife of Andrew Davidson, gardener, Newton-on-the-Moor, near Alnwick, who died on the 9th September 1873, aged 45 years. Mrs. Davidson was the author of two small volumes of poems, that show how highly she was gifted with a deep poetic feeling. Many of her best pieces were written to further the cause of temperance and political freedom ; but it is in those poems that portray her home and heart affections that we admire her most : in them we see the loving wife, the tender mother, and affectionate friend.

Dear sister, round thy narrow bed
Affection's tears will long be shed :
Thy widowed husband there will weep
And wail for thee in sorrow deep.
Oft there at twilight's peaceful hour
He'll come, his heartfelt grief to pour ;
There linger till the close of day—
Then homeward, musing, take his way.
Thy loving children there will bring
The sweetest flowers of early spring—
The primrose sweet, and snowdrop fair,
Thy once loved daisy will be there ;

Their mingled fragrance there to shed
As incense o'er thy narrow bed ;
And he who pens this heartfelt lay
A tear of memory yet will pay.
Where moulders thy once loving heart,
So free from guile in every part,
There the poetic fire did burning glow—
That heavenly flame that few can know.
But quenched for ever is that fire,
The heavenly thought, and high desire ;
But still we feel the warmth it gave,
Though thou art silent in the grave.

A CHRISTMAS SONG.

FOR LITTLE CHILDREN.

CHILDREN, loud your voices raise
In a song of thankful praise ;
This is your Saviour's natal morn,—
Jesus on this day was born.

Think of the place where He was laid,
A manger was His cradle-bed ;
And not in lordly gilded hall,
But with the tenants of the stall.

It was thus His infant life began—
The Son of God became a man ;
His life was humble here below,
A life of suffering and of woe.

"Away with Him!" His brethren cried,
And their Prince they crucified ;
" We'll have no King so vilely born !"
And they rejected Him with scorn.

But had He come in earthly state,
A mighty Conqueror, styled "The Great"—
Great in deeds of blood and strife,
Great in taking human life—

Men to Him had bowed the knee,
And thronged so great a King to see;
And given *all* to aid His cause,
And hailed His name with loud applause.

Our Lord came void of earthly state,
Yet He was the truly great;
For His friends He came to die,
And gain for them a home on high.

Now in heaven He sits a King,
And seraph hosts His praises sing;
Come, Lord, quickly to this earth again,
And subject all to Thy blest reign.

They watch in vain, the scoffers say,
For a second Advent day;
All things continue as before,
Christ to earth will come no more.

Children dear, such thoughts are vain,
Our Lord will surely come again—

Come He will, in might and power,
So watch for that dread final hour.

When you deck your home this day
With the holly and the bay,
Think where your infant Lord was laid--
In a manger cradle-bed.

Then be like Him a loving child,
Good, obedient, kind, and mild ;
All your crosses patient bear,
And Christ, your Saviour, love and fear.

COME, GENTLE SPRING.

Come, gentle spring, with all thy train,
Unloose cold winter's icy chain,
And with thy life-reviving breath
Wake Nature from the sleep of death.
Come with sunshine and with shower,
And stir to life the sleeping flower;
And to our hearts new pleasure bring,
With all the joys of early spring.

Come with all your feathered throng,
That fill our woods with joyous song;
Wake up again the dormant bee,
And clothe anew the leafless tree.
The meadows now so bleak and bare,
Clothe with grass and daisies fair;
The naked hedgerows brown and scar,
Array in greenery bright and clear.

We long to hear the cuckoo's cry,
The soaring lark sing in the sky—

Rising high on tireless wing
To welcome back the joyous spring
With all her sweet and vernal train—
The evening dew and gentle rain,
Opening buds and primrose flowers,
To deck again our woodland bowers.

Come, gentle spring, chase far away
Hoar winter in his mantle grey
Back to the frozen North again,
There to hold his court and reign.
Come, sweet spring, we long for thee
And all thy train so fair to see ;
With thankful hearts we'll gladly sing
A song of praise to thee, sweet spring.

A BALLAD

Written upon the Great Masonic Festival, given at Alnwick
Castle, upon the 8th of October 1878, by the Provincial
Grand Master, Earl Percy, M.P.

In ancient times, at Percy's call
Came Northmen staunch and true, man,
And with good sword and twanging bow
His bidding they did do, man;
With many a clout, and mighty shout,
They made his foes to fly, man;
They mowed them down like thistle-tops
When "A Percy" was the cry, man.

But times are changed since Percy ranged
From Tyne to Berwick Law, man;
Our present Earl—we proudly say't—
No foes has he at a', man.
The other day he deigned to say—
Come brethren ane and a', man,
And dine with me in the Guest Hall,
And *smoke your pipe* and a', man.

Seven hundred guests sat down to feast
In the great hall that day, man,
And such a feast before us placed
Was never seen before, man ;
When grace was sung the Earl said—
You are *welcome* ane and a', man ;
In Alnwick Castle feast this day,
The Duke invites you a', man.

Then to our feet we all did start
And hailed him with a cheer, man,
That shook the roof-tree o'er our heads—
They heard it far and near, man.
A hearty, honest, manly cheer
We gave our chief that day, man :
From our hearts that cheer came forth,
I honestly can say, man.

When every man had feasted well,
Just like a lord that day, man,
From Brother Davis in his place
Came, " Order, brethren " a', man.
Then every voice was hushed and still
In the great hall that day, man ;
Our noble Master rose and said—
Let us toast our Queen this day, man.

Then such a shout rang through the hall
For our beloved Queen, man;
That we were loyal, staunch, and true
Could easily be seen, man.
Then next he gave our *Ancient Craft*,
And he was pleased to say, man,
That it gave him pleasure in his heart
To meet us all that day, man.

Then Brother Cockcroft rose, and said
Thus to his brethren a', man—
We'll drink our noble Master's health,
May he live long and a', man,
To grace our Mystic Craft, and fill
His ancient seat and a', man;
We'll drink our noble Master's health—
We'll drink it, hip hurrah, man.

The noble Duke and Duchess' health,
And Lady Percy's too, man,
We drank in such a hearty way—
You should been there to see, man.
We waved our 'kerchiefs in the air,
And gave them three times three, man;
That some sat down for want of breath,
I very plain could see, man.

A BALLAD.

Should any Ameer or Muscovite
Give insult to our Queen, man,
We'll follow Percy to the rout,
And put her foes to shame, man.
If any craven loon at hame
Defame our Master's name, man,
We'll make his quarrel all our own,—
This justly we can claim, man.

THE FINGER-POST.

A TALE OF ALNWICK MOOR.

BEYOND the town of Alnwick, by the highway side,
There stands a finger-post, the traveller's guide;
With boards atop to tell the distance and the way,
But to what place they do not seem to say.
One board points to the north, and has a finger left;
Another southward, that is of every sign bereft:
A wretched board hangs at right angles to the post;
The one that told where Wooler lies is lost.
About this finger-post I have a tale to tell,
And this is how the thing to Willie Todd befell:
Returning from Alnwick rather late one night,
He felt not altogether just quite right;
He thought a glass or two of Peggy's "*very best*"
Would put some strength within his breast;
But alas! as he began to cross the moor
It thundered loud, and rain began to pour;
Then all at once the night became so black
That Bill saw neither moor, nor road, nor track.

He often fell, but with fresh courage rose ;
At last upon a post he struck his nose.
" Confound it ! " quoth Bill, " folk 'll think I'm
    drunk."
The words were hardly said when down he sunk.
Spent with fatigue and loss of blood
(But declared it was for want of food).
About the dawning of the day Bill wakened up,
And called for something hot and strong to sup :
" But I see," said he, " I'll not get served here ;
I am at home, that is plain and clear ;
I hear them snoring sound asleep in bed,
While I am shiv'ring by the fireside laid."
Bill started up, began to doff his coat and vest,
Then lay down, as he supposed, to rest.
Joe Prendwick with his skin cart soon passed by,
And saw beside the finger-post a half-clad body lie.
He thought at first the wretched man was dead,
And gently raised poor Willie's aching head.
Bill wakened up, and gave a heavy groan,
And called out for God's sake to be left alone.
Quoth Joe, " This is a very, very awkward case ;
I cannot leave him helpless in this wretched place ;—
I have it now : I'll wrap him in a sheep's-skin warm ;
Till I come back he'll take but little harm."
Then from his cart he took a great tup's skin,
And snugly wrapped the wretched man within.

There, like a horned sheep, our drunken hero lay,
Until Jack the shepherd chanced to stray.
He thought he saw beside the finger-post, laid fast
    asleep,
One of the freemen's black-faced sheep.
He hound his dog to drive the hungry beast away ;
The dog gave mouth and bit, but still it lay.
At length poor Bill gave forth a mighty roar,
Such as no sheep was ever heard to give before.
Quoth the shepherd, "I'll gan doon the gait and see
What sort o' beast such ugly roars can gie ;
Nae doot the beastie's starvit for want o' meat,
Or aiblins deein' frae the extraordnar' heat."
To paint the astonished wonder and surprise
That spoke from both the shepherd's eyes,
There lay no sheep, but just a great tup's skin,
With something struggling hard within.
At length poor Bill popped out his greasy head,
And asked how long he had been dead.
" Dead ?" quoth the shepherd ; "your alive as yet,
But for death or life I fear you are unfit."
Then from his shoulders he unwound his plaid,
Then in its folds the wretched man he laid,
And carried him to *good* Tom Dixon's door,
That has opened wide to many a knight before,
Belated on the wild and trackless moor,
Where winter winds in tempest pour.

Even now at times when sound asleep
Bill says he dreams of horned sheep,
And feels his heart to quake within
When he thinks upon the auld tup's skin.
Within its folds he dreamed a dream
That he dare not tell for very shame;
Since from his back the skin was cast,
He stands a man revealed at last.

MY WEE CREEPIE STOOL.*

WHAT memories surround thee, my wee creepie stool,
Linked to my childhood with its joy and dool ;
When I first left the care of kind mother's knee,
My wee creepie stool, I sate proudly on thee.

There my mother would stroke my wee flaxen head—
I'll mind her soft touch till the day that I'm dead ;
While a tear often stood in her clear sparkling e'e,
And I knew that my mother was praying for me.

From her lips I first heard of our Father above,
That His Son came to earth to teach men to love ;
Then humbly I knelt by my wee creepie stool,
And said, " Father in heaven, thy child keep and
    rule."

* A low, four-legged stool, common around the fireside in
Scottish cottages.

When the short day was done and the oil lamp was
    lit,
Entranced by the fire, on my wee stool I'd sit ;
In the glowing red embers I saw strange things
    arise—
Men, rocks, and mountains, and star-studded skies.

And strange tales I've heard on my wee creepie stool,
So strange and unearthly they made my blood cool ;
Of ghosts, and of fairies, and dead candle-lights,
And of the vile spirits that ride on dark nights.

With fear then I trembled on my wee creepie stool,
I wished for daylight with the loons at the school ;
In bed I would cover my head with the clothes,
And never feel safe till the bright sun arose.

But true pleasure I've felt on my wee creepie stool,
When my tasks were all done, and ready for school ;
Then down from the shelf came an old story-book—
To me ever new, though old it did look.

Then enraptured I read on my wee creepie stool
Of the deeds that were done when the brave Bruce
    did rule ;
At the feats of great Wallace my young blood did boil,
And I wept for his fate, when caught in the toil

At the sound of sweet music, plaintive and low,
I have sat on my stool with my heart all aglow ;
At the " Flowers o' the Forest," or "Auld Robin
    Gray,"
My heart seemed to melt, and my pulse cease to play.

When I heard the wild strains of my own dear
    Strathspey,
I danced with delight from evening to day ;
Oh ! the sweet strains of music, to man thou art given
That on earth he may foretaste the joys of heaven.

I shall never forget thee, my wee creepie stool,
For on thee I got lessons never taught me at school ;
There I learned that life to the humble and low
Has a dark dreary side that the rich never know.

Though my wee creepie stool was a low humble seat,
I have never yet envied the rich nor the great,
For life's purest pleasures are free to us all—
To the rich and the poor, to great and to small.

JOB'S RAVEN.

By the Chevy-Chase road, perched on a rail,
Job's raven sits all day wagging his tail;
And, nodding his head, he utters a croak
In the very same language his ancestors spoke.
To the lazy tramps, as they pass him by,
He screams aloud, then winks his eye;
The words he says to them I dare not write,
Nor put them down in black and white.
Job's raven can trace an unbroken descent
From the bird that from the Ark first went;
Of the time they first settled in Keilder Craig,
Tradition and history are both very vague:
But one thing is settled beyond all debate,
In days gone by they were num'rous and great;
In druidical times * we know they were there,
And lived in those days on the daintiest fare.

---

* The sacrifice offered by the druidical high priest to the gods
consisted of human victims. The most beautiful women and
children were chosen as an acceptable offering to them. They
were placed in a wicker basket suspended from the branch of a
great oak; they were there left to die—a sacrifice to the gods.

When the great high priest hung the sacrifice
On a mighty oak 'tween the earth and the skies,
Then like evil spirits in the caves of the rock
The ravens of Keilder were heard to croak;
When down they came at the dawn of day,
And carried the contents of the basket away,—
Young women and children, tender and good,
In those ancient days were their daily food.
When the Romans were here they had rich fare—
Enough, it is said, and great deal to spare;
From the Conqueror's time to the time of the
      Roses,
At common food they turned up their noses;
And during the times of Border strife,
It is said that they lived a fine jolly life.
At length there dawned the blessed day
When we ceased each other to kill and slay;
Then the ravens of Keilder had a change of fare—
Of human food their shelves were bare;
Then glad were they to find such cheer
As a dead lean sheep, or a fallen deer.
This meagre fare even failed them at last;
Then, pinched with hunger, the birds died fast:
But a small remnant still of this sable race
Strives to live on in this wild, lonely place;
The ancient halo that surrounds their name,
Appears to many but an idle dream.

A raven to them is a bird, and no more ;
A thing to be shot at, or chained at the door.
Because they are termed *birds of prey*,
The raven, forsooth, must be swept away.
If you chance to pass on the Chevy-Chase road,
Job's raven is sure to give you a nod ;
If he ruffles his feathers and wags his tail,
In his native language he is sure to rail.
The truth must be told in one single word :
Job's raven is not a *civilised* bird ;
His ideas are *radical* in the very extreme,
To every man's goods he puts in a claim.
But if Border history be valid and true,
His claims on this subject are not very new :
So, reader, if you pass on the Chevy-Chase road,
Keep your hand on your purse, and give him a nod.

F

LINES READ AT THE BURNS ANNIVERSARY,
ALNWICK.

A TOWMOND's fled since last we met
    To sing auld Scotland's praise—
Her bonnie glens and heather hills,
    Her broomy knowes and braes.
Where'er we wander, east or west,
    We never shall forget
The thicket hame, the auld fireside,
    Where we were wont to sit.

There we played around the hearth,
    Our hearts then light and free ;
There we conn'd our auld Scotch sangs,
    That ever dear will be.
Our mither sat on her laigh chair,
    And looked on the while ;
She loved to see us romp and play—
    We knew that by her smile.

There by the ingle low we read
　　Auld Scotland's stirring story ;
How Wallace wight, and Bruce the bold,
　　Upheld her ancient glory.
First there we read the wondrous tale
　　Of matchless Tam o' Shanter ;
In fancy we can see him now,
　　As he frae Ayr did canter.

Around the festive board we meet
　　To celebrate this night,
And hail again the eventful day
　　That Burns first saw the light.
That night the spirits of the air
　　Howled round the auld clay biggin' ;
The wind blew down its gable-end,
　　Stript aff the straw-thuk't riggin'.

Thus Nature hailed her darling child,
　　Her own sweet infant boy ;
She sang around his cradle-bed
　　Her wildest songs of joy.
She saw within his glowing heart
　　The latent fire divine,
Destined to light his native land,
　　And o'er the world to shine.

IN MEMORIAM OF THE EARL OF RAVENSWROTH.

The kindly man, the dear, familiar face,
We miss from the accustomed place
Where he was wont to kneel in prayer,
As lowly as the humblest there.
His loving heart, his tongue of fire,
Lies silent like a broken lyre ;
No more he'll see with rapturous eyes
The new-blown flowers from earth arise ;
No more he'll tread the heath-clad hill,
Nor rest beside the murmuring rill ;
No more at eventide he'll stray
Along the path and hidden way,
There to forget all earthly care,
And muse with God and Nature there.
A man of high and cultured mind,
He loved his country and his kind ;
For Britain's rights, his country's good,
He like a patriot staunchly stood ;

His duty clear, then nought could move
If conscience bade him to approve;
Careless alike of censure or applause,
He staunchly stuck to Britain's cause.
Such was the man we miss and mourn,
Gone from our sight ne'er to return;
Left us in the early days of spring,
When Nature forth her treasures bring;
But loving hands its flowers will spread,
And strew them round his peaceful bed.

ALONE.

"I will make him an help meet for him."

Man in Paradise was placed,
There Nature's choicest gifts to taste ;
Lovely birds with plumage fair
Sang to their mates, and sported there ;
Every creature did true pleasure find
In loving union with its kind ;
But the man *alone* was there,
Until God gave him Eve so fair,
To be a help meet, loving, kind,
In all a reflex of his mind ;
There she a beauteous woman shone,
"Flesh of his flesh, bone of his bone."
When to-day you at the altar stand
And take your husband by the hand,
May your hearts united be,
Close as the branch is to the tree ;
Long may you thus together live,
To taste the joy that wedded life can give.

MY LITTLE PRIMROSE FLOWER.

THERE grows a golden primrose
   In a lone mossy dell,
The place where grows my primrose
   I'll not to any tell ;
Beneath the shelter of an oak,
   That's wrinkled grey with age,
My pet flower blossoms sweetly there,
   Safe from the tempest's rage.

A little rill that trickles by
   Makes music to my flower,
And wafts itself in dewy spray
   To cool its mossy bower.
The speckled trout leap up with joy
   When bright it shines and clear,
And April brings its gentle rain
   My little flower to cheer.

Spring wakens Nature from her sleep,
   There little birds do sing,
To see the trees put forth their buds,
   And flowers begin to spring.

The robin makes his cosy nest
　　Beside my little flower,
And close beneath its shelt'ring leaves
　　His little brood does cower.

When in the west the evening star
　　Shines like a diamond bright,
The feathered choir in brake and briar
　　Sing sweet their last good-night;
And ere the morning star has sunk
　　Behind the Cheviots grey,
They sing to my flower in its mossy bower
　　Their hymn to the coming day.

At morning dawn a sunbeam steals
　　Where my pet flower is laid,
And wakes it with a warm soft kiss
　　Upon its golden head.
My virgin flower, like maiden pure,
　　Lifts its head to the azure sky,
And wafts perfume from its golden bloom
　　On the breeze that passes by.

Then come the bees through budding trees;
　　With a hum of joy they sing
To the flower of my little primrose,
　　The queen of early spring;

From its cup of gold they sip
  The honey sweet and clear,
And carry home with joyous song
  The first-fruits of the year.

As 'neath this old oak-tree I sit,
  I think of boyhood's day,
When, spotless as the primrose flower.
  On the sunny bank I lay :
I gazed from earth to vaulted sky,
  Till I seemed borne away
To a land of bliss, unlike to this,
  Where flowers know no decay.

LINES WRITTEN ON A VISIT TO SPEYSIDE.

WHEN tired with worldly cares and toil,
    How pleasant 'tis to stray,
And taste the sweets that Nature spreads
    Along the banks of Spey !
No music to my ear so dear
    As thine, soft murm'ring stream !
The memory of it haunts my heart
    Like some forgotten dream.

Though life's young day has passed away,
    With all its fancied train
Of boyish hopes and airy dreams,
    Yet thou art still the same.
Oft on thy sandy banks I built
    The mimic castle high,
And tried, like ancient Bab'lon's sons,
    To reach the vaulted sky.

But sandy castles are like those
    We build high in the air—
They vanish like the morning mist,
    And leave our landscape bare.

Ah! where are now the hearts and hands
    That joined my boyish play?
Some on life's stream have gone to wreck,
    And some have passed away.

A few, like men, fight bravely in
    Life's battle, sorely prest;
But onward, upward, still they cry,
    "We'll conquer ere we rest."
Oft to the earth they are borne down,
    And forced to quit the field;
But still aloft Hope's banner waves
    With "Die, but never yield!"

Ye greyhaired fathers of my youth,
    I'll meet you here no more;—
Just like a stream, in years gone by
    You've reached the boundless shore.
Yonder, around the grey kirk walls,
    Your final rest you take;
To earthly change and busy life
    No coming morn will wake.

The Sunday bell that tolls at morn
    Will greet your ears no more;
Alas! no more your friends you'll meet
    Around the old kirk door;

In friendly talk no more you'll join,
    Nor ever want to know
If beasts be selling cheap or dear,
    Or grain priced high or low.

Sons of the soil! your life was toil,
    But softly now ye rest,
And sleep as soundly and as calm
    As those in purple dressed.
Upon yon crumbling moss-grown stones
    I read your name and age,
With many a solemn warning text
    Culled from the sacred page.

Your simple lives need no historic pen,
    No brazen trumpet to rehearse your fame;
Your humble virtues long will live behind,
    Though flatt'ring record never breathe your
        name.
Yours were the virtues that made Scotland great—
    A frugal people and united state;
When tyrants rose to hurl you from your seat,
    Them back ye thrust in sure and dire defeat.

BLIND HECTOR AND HIS DOG.

LED by his faithful dog from door to door,
Blind Hector wandered many a parish o'er :
No beggar he ; although by bounty fed,
He never had to ask for clothes or bread --
All had a welcome for the blind old man.
With shouts of glee the children ran,
And strove who first should lead away,
As guest, the hero of the day.
His faithful Tyke, that seemed possessed
Of more than kindness in his breast,
His blind old master's friend and guide,
That never changed nor left his side—
Unlike those friends that soon grow cold,
If we are wretched, poor, and old—
The faithful dog no meanness knew,
And had no sordid aims in view.
Along the rough uneven street
He careful led the blind man's feet,
Knew every house along the way,
Knew where to call and where to stay ;
And well he knew their night's retreat,
With " Hector's Corner " and his seat,

Where oft he'd sat, a welcome guest,
To Sunday fare and Christmas feast.
And when the earth lay wrapped in snow,
He sat beside the peat-fire's glow,
And to the listening ploughmen told
Tales of his clansmen brave and bold,—
Of dark Culloden's murd'rous fray,
Where chief and clansmen vanquished lay,
And he himself fell in the van,
Amongst the bravest of his clan,
And crawled from thence at dead of night,
A wounded man with loss of sight,
And from that day he forth did roam
An exile from his mountain home.
For forty years a wand'rer's life he led,
And nightly filled a beggar's bed;
On rough-made bed of straw or hay
For forty years the blind man lay;
And ere his homely couch he prest,
A solemn prayer rose from his breast,
With thanks for mercies kindly given
By his Almighty Friend in heaven;
Then calm he laid him down to rest,
With not a murmur in his breast.

But mishap on the best will fall,
And come alike on great and small.

One luckless morn they chanced to meet
A cur upon the village street,
Who sprang on Tyke in sudden ire.
Quick as a spark shoots from the fire,
The blind man raised his trusty stick,
Therewith the savage beast to strike,
But struck poor Tyke the deadly blow
Was meant to lay his rival low.
The poor old dog gave one low groan
That told his parting breath had gone ;
A wail rose from the old man's breast,
As in his arms he fondly prest
The lifeless dog, his friend and guide,
Whom nought could tempt to leave his side.
Quick to the scene the neighbours ran,
And kindly soothed the poor old man ;
A farmer took poor Hector home,
And from his roof he ne'er did roam,
While age and sorrow soon him laid
Where none need human help or aid.
Beneath yon ash, with berries red,
We laid blind Hector's old grey head ;
And just beyond the crumbling wall,
Where soft the leaves in autumn fall,
The children made poor Tyke a grave,
And over both the branches wave.

LINES INSCRIBED TO WILLIAM GREEN, ESQ., RUTHRIE.

Accept, dear sir, this homely rhyme,
Though rude in measure and in chime ;
My grateful heart would speak your praise
For kindness done in bygone days.
You kindly helped me when a boy,
And filled my heart with secret joy :
I longed to leave our hills behind,
And mingle freely with my kind :
Hope pointed with her magic wand
To the longed-for and blessèd land—
A land all seek, but none have found—
The place where nought but joys abound.
But I have found, what some may miss,
A friend to share life's ills and bliss.
Nigh thirty years have passed away
Since I beneath your roof-tree lay,
And many a change has passed since then
O'er barren moor and lonely glen.
Where grew the broom and stunted thorn,
There now waves rich the yellow corn ;

Where nought but barren heath was seen,
The eye rests now on richest green.
Such is the change I now can trace
Around your erewhile well-known place :
By energy and skilful toil,
You've made the wilderness to smile.
But sad's the change that I can see
On many a face long known to me :
Ay ! many a face once smooth and fair
Is wrinkled now and marked with care ;
And many a friend I loved to meet
I miss from off the village street.

But why should I pursue this theme ?
The past is gone like fairy dream :
It's for the present we must live,
And to its wants our thoughts must give ;
And if the sceptic's tale be true,
Men need no higher aim pursue.
We live (say they) to eat and drink,
And then in dark oblivion sink.
This is the doctrine that they preach,
Though scarce believe they what they teach.
Man longs for some more healing balm,
To soothe life's ills, and shed a calm
On his strange, fitful, troubled life,
So full of cares and aimless strife.

In vain he asks his fellow-man
T' unriddle life's mysterious plan ;
He tries, but only tries in vain,
Our life's deep purpose to explain.
We see around us sin and care,
Pale misery and dark despair,
And wanton luxury and pride
Flaunt gaily past the beggar's side ;
Men spending life in vain debate
For party names, at best a *cheat*,
That stir men's passions into strife,
That blights and poisons all their life.
We see the bloody demon War
Ride on triumphant in his car,
And lay whole nations in the dust
To satiate men's pride and lust ;
And *liberty* seems but a dream—
Men only know it yet by name ;
And in its name such deeds are done,
As make us blush before the sun !
Men call it liberty to break the laws
Of heaven and earth to aid their cause,
To trample every sacred trust
That men hold holy in the dust.
And shall we look and long in vain
For that blest time when love shall reign ?
No happier world will greet our view
While men their selfish aims pursue.

But from these thoughts I gladly turn
To your bright home beside the burn,
Where life so peaceful glides away,
Calm as the eve of summer's day.
Around you Nature, charming wild,
Seems ever changing like a child ;
Each passing day spreads to your view
Old scenes that every hour seem new.
At once we turn our wandering eyes
To Benrinne's top, that meets the skies,
And mark his ever-changing form
Amidst the sunshine and the storm.
The lesser hills that meet our view
Seem ever changing in their hue.
Along the winding vale of Spey
A thousand beauties lure the eye ;
The waving pine-woods, dark and green,
Lend varied glory to the scene ;
And over all there seems to rest
A calm that soothes the troubled breast,
That bids our anxious cares to cease
Where all around breathes calm and peace.
Even now my thoughts will often turn
To rocky linn and winding burn,
Where I have wandered free from care,
And happy as the birds of air.
My soul, at one with all around,
Drank in each pleasant sight and sound :

The breeze that broke the evening calm
Made music like some heavenly psalm,
That wafts the spirit up on high,
Far from the scenes that round us lie,—
When to the soul a glimpse is given
And foretaste of the bliss of heaven.
Sweet Nature! source of purest joy!
Thou sooth'st my heart when cares annoy:
Oft have I felt thy magic power
In life's dark melancholy hour.
Grant me, O Heaven! some lonely glen,
Far from the toil and strife of men;
There let me live and let me die
Beneath God's clear and azure sky;
And when this doubting spirit's fled,
Let me be with the lowly laid,
That 'neath the green sod nameless lie,
But whose fair record is on high.
And while I live I'll grateful be
For all your kindness shown to me;
And may the dove-like angel Peace
Your home make sacred and your place,
Where you have reared, with taste and skill,
A charming villa on the hill,
Where you and your belovèd wife
May peaceful spend the eve of life;
And when you've finished life's brief day,
God grant you higher joys, I pray.

AUTUMN.

Who loves not Autumn's short'ning day
Through fruitful fields and lanes to stray,
And list the plaintive redbreast sing,
Where we have spent life's early spring?
With joy we turn our wondering eye
On the fair scenes that round us lie,
On golden fields of ripened grain,
Matured by Summer's sun and rain.

Sweet scents come wafted on the breeze,
From clover-fields and forest-trees;
Nature her incense casts abroad
O'er hill and plain and dusty road;
And smiling Autumn scatters wide
A bounteous store on every side,
And crowns man's labour and his toil
With generous plenty from the soil.

All Nature seems to feel decay,
And calmly waits to *pass away,*

Like some great spirit, bless'd and pure,
That smiling waits the final hour
To cast aside earth's cumbrous load,
And upward wing its flight to God,
To join the ransomed throng above,
Where all is joy and peace and love.

Who has not felt the soothing power
Of Autumn's silent twilight hour?
The great moon, like a golden shield,
Casts magic light o'er hill and field;
A calm sweet peace seems shed abroad,
That lifts the spirit up to God—
To Him to whom our hearts should rise,
Who rules all nature, earth, and skies.

Creatures that shun the light of day
Come forth at eve to sport and play;
The owl and night-hawk seek their food
Through the green fields that skirt the wood;
The timorous hare and rabbit shy
Hide in the grass as we pass by;
And moths and insects, painted fair,
Float joyous through the evening air.

The noise of youth at evening play
Comes from the village up the way,

And happy groups we ofttimes meet,
Singing in chorus low and sweet ;
Perchance love song or Border lay
Wakes echoes from yon ruin grey,
Where once the nightly warders trod,
To guard from foes their rude abode.

The caw of rooks from Shawdon's trees
Comes floating on the rising breeze ;
For ages there they've found retreat
In Winter's cold and Summer's heat :
A Father's bounty doth their needs supply
From those fair vales that round them lie ;
They have no garners flowing o'er
With golden grain for Winter's store.

An ancient steeple meets our eyes
Above the mist that round it lies,
A grey cold mist, that seems to weep
O'er those beneath, that silent sleep ;
They wait for that dread solemn hour
When God shall raise them by His power.

IN MEMORY OF THE LATE MRS. IBBOTSON,

BELOVED WIFE OF THE REV. MR. IBBOTSON, GREAT AYTON, CLEVELAND, YORKSHIRE.

" Being dead, yet speaketh."

LIKE to a rose whose fallen bloom
Sends up to heaven its rich perfume ;
The fallen leaves that withered lie,
Waft their sweet incense to the sky.

Meet type of her whose loss we mourn,
Whose spirit now has crossed that bourn,
And entered where they are at rest
Whom earthly cares no more molest.

No outward badge of Christ she wore,
But in her heart the cross she bore ;
Her soul o'erflowed with gentle love
For men below and God above.

She watched the young with tender care
From every vile and hurtful snare,
And strove to guide them on the road
That leads to happiness and God.

Her call was not " aloud to cry "
To giddy throng that hurries by ;
But, with a woman's gentle love,
She tried their thoughtless hearts to move.

For all she sent the secret prayer
To Him who makes mankind His care,
That He would send the Spirit down,
His own bless'd work on earth to crown.

All earthly things she " counted loss ; "
She only lived to bear the cross,
Which she on earth has now laid down,
To wear in heaven her promised crown.

TIME, LIKE A RIVER, ROLLS ALONG!

WRITTEN ON NEW YEAR'S DAY.

Oh! deem it not a vain or idle dream :
We all are sailors on this mighty stream.
Another noted landmark now is passed ;
To many voyagers it may prove the last.
But let us look around upon the throng
Of fellow-voyagers as we sail along.
See yonder, now a gallant bark appears ;
With steady hand and sure the helmsman steers ;
Mark with what care he passed the sunken rock,
On which full many a gallant bark has broke.
Though beacons shed abroad their warning light
To guide the mariner's dark course aright,
Some careless steer, and, with unwatchful eye
To mark and see where hidden dangers lie,
Unconscious of their course, they sail along,
And spend the night with heedless mirth and song,
Until, at last, they strike some hidden reef,
Where human power can seldom give relief –

The fatal rocks where thousands daily fall :
Some term them passion, some intemp'rance call :
But from them you may hear the wretched cry
For help from man, or mercy from on high,
When, sailing smooth, they spurn the light of Heaven.
To guide the voyager's course that light was given :
This light the watchful mariner descries,
And ever keeps as pole-star in his eyes.
When tempests roar, and darkness clouds the night,
The compass guides him on his course aright :
His chart tells where the hidden rocks abound,
Where foaming breakers dash with sullen sound.
He knows he sails the dang'rous deep,
And is for ever watchful not to sleep.
But hark ! now as he glides along
And turns his sails with joyous song,
He feels his heart rise with the breeze,
And in each cloud new beauty sees :
He sees the banks in beauty drest,
Where all seem happy—all seem blest ;
Each passing headland brings to view
Scenes ever varied, ever new.
At last a dim haze meets his eyes,
He knows that there the ocean lies.
Long has he wished upon its breast
To strike his sails and be at rest ;
But ah ! the dang'rous bar—it must be crossed,
Where many a noble bark's been lost.

To pierce the gloom he strains his eye—
Hark ! hark ! he hears the Pilot cry !
Joy of all joys ! with beating, trustful heart
He yields the helm to His unerring art !

THE BLIND MAN'S DREAM.

Oh! lead me forth, my own sweet child!
    The sun, you say, shines bright;
I love to feel his warming rays,
    Though I cannot see his light.

Oh! lead me to the green turf-seat,
    Beneath the old ash-tree;
And then, my child, you'll join your mates;
    I love to hear your glee.

I'd rather hear your merry laugh,
    So happy and so wild,
Than be by sensuous revelry
    In pleasure's haunts beguiled.

Oh! how I love to hear your laugh,
    So full of happy glee!
Oh! the glad mem'ries it revives,
    Memories dear to me!

Oh! can it be my eyeballs dim
　　Have got their wonted light,
And here again on earth I see
　　Her angel form so bright?

I do not wish her here again,
　　Where all is care and woe,
But rather would I join her there,
　　And to her bright world go.

I see her beckon with her hand,
　　I hear her whisp'ring say,
" Why do you linger here below?
　　Haste, haste, and come away!"

Methinks I see her lovely face
　　With more than beauty shine,
A dazzling light around it plays,
　　A beauty all divine.

Is this a vision of my brain,
　　That seems to float in light?
For round her is a glorious train,
　　Familiar to my sight.

I thought I heard her mellow voice
　　Sound high a heavenly theme:
A child's sweet voice my slumber broke,
　　Alas! I did but dream.

HEART MEMORIES.

THERE are mem'ries treasured in the heart
  Which tongue hath never told,
Nor would their rich possessors sell
  For worlds of glittering gold.
Our sacred treasure's guarded fast,
  With more than miser care ;
We would not our bright gems display
  To the rude world's stare.

The heart that has no mem'ries dear
  Is like an empty spring,
Which to the weary trav'ller's heart
  No healing waters bring.
But he whose soul is stored with these
  Has more than jewels rare :
He carries daily in his heart
  A cure for biting care.

When tired of life's steep rugged road,
  He cheers his weary way

With mem'ries sweet of days long past,
   That seem but yesterday.
Perchance the forms of dear old friends
   Up in review he brings;
They pass through memory's golden gate
   On soft and downy wings.

But there's a form, when all is fled,
   That ne'er doth pass away,
To mem'ry's eye 'tis never lost
   The livelong night and day.
Oft has that form brought peace and hope
   Back to the troubled heart,
And made the tears of bliss and joy
   Unconsciously to start.

The soft sweet tear of memory,
   Like blessèd summer rain,
Quickens the dried-up weary heart.
   And bids it smile again.
Who has not felt the soothing power
   Of mem'ry's soft'ning tear,
When into that rich treasure-house
   We enter without fear?

THE EXILE'S RETURN.

Come, my Jeanie, let us wander
By yon fairy-haunted stream ;
It warbles sweet as when we parted
In the days of youth's sweet dream.

Oft when I was lonely straying
On a far, far distant shore,
Here in fancy I was roaming
With you as in days of yore.

When silent eve, with noiseless step,
Came creeping o'er the lonely deep ;
By its murm'ring shore I wandered
Till Nature's voice was hushed in sleep.

And when I pressed my lonely couch,
In dreams I wandered far away ;
I gambolled on the village green,
Or on the lonely banks of Spey.

II

And when the morning's downy light
   Crept up the sky on golden wing,
Then all the birds in chorus woke,
   And made the air with music ring.

'Twas not the song of that dear thrush
   That sounds so sweet from yonder tree,
Nor yet the ringdove's am'rous note,
   Whose ev'ning song is dear to me;

Nought could cheer my drooping heart,
   'Twas like a withered, sapless tree;
I longed to tread my native heath,
   And see my Jane, so dear to me.

Never more shall riches tempt me
   With its empty glittering store;
Never more I'll wander from thee,
   Nor quit again my native shore.

HASTE TO THE BRIDAL.

WRITTEN ON THE MARRIAGE OF LORD LORNE TO THE PRINCESS LOUISE.

GATHER, gather, men of the heather,
Haste ye all to the bridal this day!
    Our young chief of Lorne
    We'll toast high this morn,
And wish him great joy this day.
    Our clan feuds are ended,
    Our best breath we'll spend it,
And shout for the Campbells, hurrah! hurrah!

Gather, gather! we'll muster and pray
For joy to the daughter of Albert this day.
    Bride of a nation!
    High is your station;
You're wedded to ever-true Scotland this day.
    Our best blood we'll spend it,
    Your hearth to defend it,
And shout for the Campbells, hurrah! hurrah!

Like our mountain-pine and heather,
May you both live long together;

Your hearts closer twining
As life keeps declining,
May your love never fade nor decay.
This life may you spend it,
That in peace you may end it,
Every true Scottish heart will pray, will pray,
For our young couple this day—this day.

Gather, gather, the loyal and true,
Men of the plaid and bonnets of blue ;
Our mountain-tops high
Shall echo your cry
Of "God save our Queen" this day.
'Mid cares that annoy,
May the thought give her joy,
That a nation loves her this day, this day,
Who for their dear Sovereign will pray, will pray.

Our Queen loves her home 'mong the heather,
There sweet memories round her gather,
Of days that are past and gone,
When she walked not alone,
But Albert by her side did stray,
Whose gentle spirit still
Seems to haunt each glen and hill,
Where our Queen loves to stray, to stray,
And spend there the sweet Autumn day.

BELL THE CAT:

A CHRISTMAS TALE FOR LITTLE CHILDREN.

(Written at the request of a little boy.)

MILLER WHITTLE was just what a miller should be,
He sung like a blackbird and worked like a bee.
First thing in the morning the hopper he'd fill,
Then he went to the race and set on the mill ;
The water rushed down with a dash and a splash,
And the mill went to work with a rumbling crash.
Clack, clack ! went the hopper, and down came the
    meal,
Then off singing to breakfast the miller would steal,
His face shining red like ripe cherries in June,
Transparent like amber and covered with bloom :
His eyes had a twinkle of good-humoured glee,
That spoke of a kind heart you plainly could see.
To all folks alike he was loving and kind,
His equal in England you hardly could find.
The beggars all round found their way to the mill,
For they knew that the miller their meal-bags would fill ;

To the lame and the lazy, the vile and the good,
He gave a night's shelter and plenty of food ;
The ewes on the hill would come bounding with glee,
And they bleated with pleasure the miller to see,
For a sieve full of corn he often would bring,
And feed them like children arranged in a ring ;
While the pigs on their hind-legs looked over the stye,
And grunted with rapture whene'er he came nigh :
Hens, ducks, and pigeons flocked by the score,
To be fed by the miller round the mill-door.

Most men have a dislike to this thing or to that,
And the miller he hated the sight of a cat ;
So the mice at the mill had it all their own way,
And did as they liked both by night and by day ;
For they feasted like lords on his milk and his meal,
And butter and cheese they did wantonly steal.
Oft at night when the miller went snugly to rest,
They would creep into bed and lie down on his
        breast.
One night, as he lay 'tween a sleep and a doze,
He felt a wee mousie fast eating his nose ;
Then he shouted aloud, " Wifey, strike up a light !
My own canny woman, I have had a sore fright.
It is blood, wife, ay, truly ! what say you to that ?
They will soon take our lives if we don't get a cat.
If they let me see morning with the sight of my eyes,
I'll make them repent ere the sun leaves the skies."

So the old miller borrowed, the very next day,
Lame Lizzy's tom-cat, all so glossy and grey.
Tom scanned his new home with a grave solemn air,
And looked as important 's a clown at a fair.
Refreshed with new milk he sat stroking his beard,
When a scuffle and squeak in the chamber was heard.
Tom said to himself, " My old friends are up there ! "
Then quickly as lightning he mounted the stair.
The mice fled before him like the fast-fleeting wind,
But a dozen met death that no refuge could find.
The news (like ill news) were soon spread through the
    mill,
And dismay and terror each mouse heart did fill ;
It was said that a creature with fire-flashing eyes
Had dropped to devour them direct from the skies ;
Some said it walked, and some declared that it flew,
But no mouse could escape it, they very well knew.
'Mongst the mice at the mill there was fear and dismay,
As pining with hunger in their dark holes they lay,
And the tears from their little dark bead-eyes did
    steal,
As they thought of the past with its milk and its meal,
And the sweet hours they 'd spent in revel and play,
Dancing and romping through the mill night and day.
At last they resolved that a meeting take place,
To consider some means to improve their sad case ;
So while Tom took his nap in the miller's arm-chair,
The mice held their meeting in trembling and fear.

In an empty old meal-kist the meeting took place,
Where no preying cat could present his foul face.
Then Alderman Mouseman was called to the chair;
When he rose up to speak all gave a loud cheer.
The chairman stood up on a billet of wood
That in corner of meal-kist luckily stood.
He said, " I see mice here with talent and skill,
Who could state far more clearly our rights to the
        mill ;
For *we* have a right, that I'll boldly maintain,
To do as we like with the meal and the grain.
What is this *here* miller but a tenant-at-will,
With no legal right to his means or his mill ?
But our rights from our fathers we clearly can trace,
Who for ages have lived upon this *here* place.
I see our friend Councillor Fieldmouse is here,
And he is the man that can make our case clear."
Then Councillor Fieldmouse stood up and said, " Hem !
I feel, Mr. Chairman, as if in a dream ;
I cannot find words that would fully express
How deeply I feel our sad state and distress.
You all know, my friends, how this matter arose :
Some young thoughtless mouse bit the old miller's
        nose ;
For this, the old tyrant is going to kill
Every *bit* mouse in his house and his mill.
I now call on this meeting to join as one mouse,
To drive this vile man from his mill and his house ;

And I am sure, my dear friends, you are all well aware,
That we must move in this matter with caution and care.
This vile wicked cat by some means we must kill,
Before we are masters of the house or the mill."
Then old Madam Shrewmouse bawled out with a
    squeak,
" Will you allow, Mr. Chairman, an old female to speak ?
I hate all palavers, with your hums and your haws :
There is no need for caution in such a good cause.
If you only will act upon what I suggest,
And deprive the old miller of comfort and rest ;
I would tease and torment him by night and by day,
I would scratch out his eyes while sleeping he lay,
His bags in the mill to shreds I would tear,
And leave him no atom of clothing to wear ;
For such tyrants as he ought never to live :
So kill him at once is the advice that I give ;
But if any one thinks he can better my plan,
Let him stand up on his legs and speak out like a man."
Then up started young Fopmouse with fine swelling
    dash,
He bowed to the chair, and then stroked his moustache,
And said, " Mr. Chairman, and all present here,
The whole thing, to my mind, is easy and clear :
This vile wicked cat is our deadliest foe,
And never is seen till he deals a death-blow.
' A cat has nine lives,' I have heard people say,
And sees better in darkness than ev'n in day.

If we could tie round his neck a small tinkling bell,
It would ring when he moved, and his coming would
    tell.
Now, my worthy friends all, what say you to that?"
With one voice they shouted, "Bell the cat! bell the
    cat!"
Then said old Father Dormouse, hoary with age,
"Friends, listen to me, for I've lived in a cage.
Hodge, my first owner, was a labourer meek,
Who prayed by proxy just once every week;
He fed me with crumbs and the best that he had,
But said that the world in general was bad.
For riches and wealth he felt no great desire,
But would have been glad if his wages were higher;
Not that he cared for wealth or very rich food,
But riches would give him the means to do good.
This Hodge had a love both for nature and art,
And could tell how far heaven and earth were apart;
He knew all the laws that regulate force,
And said the same power ruled a planet and horse.
He kept me, he said, to enlighten his mind,   .
And to prove if old age caused the mouse to grow blind.
One day to his cottage a pious lady came in.
And said, 'Don't you think it a very great sin
To keep a poor mouse shut up in this way,
Exposed to the light and sunshine of day?
For they are like sinners, who love not the light,
And do all their deeds in the darkness of night.'

'Mam,' said old Hodge, 'it is just as you say,
Mice were made for the night, and not for the day.
For we see in all nature a purpose and plan,
All guided by rule save the offspring of man.'
'Hodge, a right clever man you are in your way,'
And the lady wished Hodge and his wife a good day.
That hour, Mr. Chairman, my knowledge began
Of the world in gen'ral, of woman and man;
For the very next day by Hodge I was sold
To a trav'lling showman for sovereign in gold.
The showman (as he called it) put me to school,
And taught me to act by square and by rule.
Poised on my hind-legs, he taught me to stand,
Dressed like a parson in cassock and band;
Then I pretended to read, in a droll squeaking way,
With specks on my nose to bow and to sway;
Then dressed like a fop in the very first style,
With my pipe, a switch and a fash'nable *tile*,
Smoothing my beard, I strolled slowly along,
Humming the tune of a doggerel song.
I soon became known as 'the wonderful mouse,'
And drew to my master many a full house.
'Ladies and gentlemen,' 'twas his custom to say,
'Here now is a sight seldom seen in our day;
This wonderful creature's the white mouse of Moab,
Common in the days of the patriarch Job.
This *here* is the species, I am credibly told,
The Philistines fashioned and carved out in gold;

Brought to this country by traveller last year,
I bought it, I assure you, at a price very dear.
Ladies and gentlemen, see this *fact* with your eyes,
I'm not like quack doctors who tell nothing but lies.'
My life, Mr. Chairman, was a burden to me,
I need not tell how much I longed to be free.
One night as we drove down a very steep hill,
The van was upset and I escaped to the mill;
From slavery and bondage to liberty dear,
You don't know the contrast, that is very clear.
My friends, I advise you to alter your plan,
And respect the old miller, for he's a good man."
At this sage advice there were hisses and cries
Of "Down with old Dormouse, and blacken his eyes!
He knows nought of life but the vulgar and low,
And has spent all his time in a travelling show."
'Midst all this confusion and wildest uproar,
The miller and Tom came in at the door;
They both heard the noise that came from the kist,
And fell on the mice ere ever they wist.
A good hearty kick, with a push and a thrust,
Sent all the pack flying—the old kist to dust;
The miller laid round him with hearty good-will,
While Tom did his work with calmness and skill.

Now the miller sleeps soundly, free from all fear,
And Tom does the same in the old arm-chair.

Thus the mice were like some little folks we've seen,
That are never content—you may know who I mean ;
They want to have something they do not possess,
Perhaps a new suit or a fine muslin dress ;
And then, like the mice, they fall into mischief,
Which is sure to end quickly in sorrow and grief.
There are some bigger children, whose hair is nigh grey,
That are never content with the times, as they say ;
With them, nothing is right, but everything wrong,—
This cannot last long, is their chorus and song.

Now, dear children all, I have a last word to say,
Be sure to get *wisdom* before you grow grey ;
And when merry at Christmas and Happy New Year,
May your best friends be there to enjoy your good cheer !

"THE KAIL BROSE O' AULD SCOTLAND."

Let English chiels their roast-beef crack,
    Their puddings plump, and a' that;
We'll ne'er despise our lang-kail brose,
    For beef we canna fa that.
They sneer and laugh at Sawny's taste
    For crowdy, brose, and a' that;
Say they, " We'll eat his black-faced sheep,
    And gie 'm the *head* to chaw at."

Nae doubt we send them nowt and sheep,
    Our pigs and hens, and a' that;
But aye keep fat to grease our sheen,
    And taste our gabs, and a' that.
When Yule comes roun', we get our fill
    O' flesh and fish, and a' that,
And ance or twice throughout the year,
    But aftener canna fa that.

An Englishman gets roast and boiled,
    Wi' puddings het, and a' that;

And then he maun hae beer to drink,
   An' no content wi' a' that.
But then we get our 'taties het,
   Boiled in their skins, an' a' that ;
And maybe whiles a herring sma',
   But seldom we can fa that.

But can they boast mair sturdy chiels,
   Fed on their beef and a' that,
Than we can do, fed on kail brose,
   On crowdy, broth, and a' that ?
I winna boast our hasty brose,
   Our stir-about, and a' that ;
They may do when they're butter'd nice,
   Wi' pepper, salt, and a' that.

They ca' our porridge, wi' sour-milk,
   But fit for pigs, and a' that ;
But then we canna grease our beards
   Wi' butter'd toast, and a' that.
Our lairds themsells can only get
   Beef, pudding, toast, and a' that ;
If we would eat sic dainties nice,
   They'd raise our rents, and a' that.

Let Frenchmen eat their frogs an' mice,
   Their nasty stews, and a' that ;

And Paddy boast his 'taties nice,
    Wi' butter-milk, and a' that;
And Johnnie Bull may eat his full
    Of beef and pork, and a' that;
A heapit bicker o' kail brose,
    Is Scotland's yet, for a' that.

LINES WRITTEN ON THE FIELD OF CULLODEN.

(DEDICATED TO SAUNDERS M'GREGOR, WHOSE GREAT-
GRANDFATHER FELL ON THAT MEMORABLE DAY.)

DARK lowered the night, the morn was grey
That ushered in Culloden's day—
That day of blood, and hate, and strife,
When man from man sought life for life.

Oh! could my muse like Ossian's tell
How clansmen fought, how foemen fell,
And how the Saxons, clad in steel,
Before their foes were made to reel—

Reeled as a bark by tempest tossed,
A moment seen, then all is lost—
Lost in the billowy surge of war:
Their deafening yell was heard afar.

Oh ! need I tell how chieftains led,
And for their Prince like martyrs bled ?
Or need I tell how dauntless they
Against such odds urged on the fray ?

How oft above the battle-yell
Each gathering cry was heard to swell ;
And like a lion pressed for life,
Each cheered his followers to the strife ?

See yon proud host, when conscious they
By numbers great must gain the day !
See how their hate impels them on !
Their rallying-cry is, " Quarter ?   None ! "

What ear can listen, tongue rehearse,
Their deeds ?—'twould stain the vilest verse.
Then let their leader's blasted name
From age to age be crowned with shame !

See yon proud host who never fled !
See how they're on by heroes led !
Death unto them has terrors none,
If their dear country's honour's gone !

But, ah! that day the fates had sworn
That few so brave should see the morn :
Though brave they fought and nobly fell—
That dire defeat should ring their knell.

Oh! here let Scotia drop a tear
For those brave sons she held so dear!
Dear to their country is their name—
They long shall be her minstrels' theme.

LOVE AND FRIENDSHIP.

FRIENDSHIP and Love conjointly claim
The same pure essence, but a diff'rent name.
But what have they in common?   Search and
    see ;
To find a likeness puzzles me.
Love, like a playful, thoughtless child,
Often by fancy is beguiled.
And see how oft the silly thing
Will to a lady's ringlets cling ;
Even the glancing of an eye
Will make his maddened pulse beat high.
Sometimes a red and pimpled nose
His godship in hysterics throws ;
Ay ! ev'n a crimson bloated cheek
Will keep him bedfast for a week.
Why should we blush to speak the truth ?
The deadliest weapon is the mouth ;
Though like a snake with death it's fraught,
The silly fool longs for the draught ;
He tastes, and feels the deadly smart
Of lurking poison at his heart.

Sometimes he is like amorous dove,
A shining neck will fatal prove ;
Round it you see him fondly cling,
Just like a bat on outstretched wing.
Oft has a slender taper waist
Upset his godship's sweetest rest ;
Ev'n worse than that, in wild despair
He's cut life's thread to ease his care.
Look down, ye powers ! and blush to see 't,
His godship at a lady's feet ;
Grovelling, fast to them he clings,
Though in the dust he soil his wings.
Friendship, be mine ; I claim your hand,
And swear by you to fall or stand :
To me more dear thy friendly grip
Than all the talk of Cupid's lip.

EARL PERCY'S WEDDING-DAY.

MEN of Alnwick ! shout and sing
Till our castle turrets ring ;
Earl Percy home a flower will bring
   He has pulled this day,
A tender, blooming, sweet young thing
   Off the mountains grey.

God 'fend his bonny heather-bell,
And bring her safe to lowland dell ;
May sons unborn yet joyful tell
   Of this happy day ;
God shield them from misfortunes fell,
   From our hearts we pray.

May Percy bless to 's latest hour
The day he culled his Highland flower,
And brought her to his English bower,
   His heart's best treasure ;
May dark misfortune's clouds ne'er lower
   To spoil their pleasure.

Flower of an ancient glorious stock !
Child of the *mist* and mountain rock !
Your ancient tree oft bore war's shock
   And felt the blow,
But still stood firm when others broke,
   And now lie low.

The name of your great martyred sire *
Stirs in our hearts the latent fire :
To such a name may you aspire
   In future story ;
God shield you from a fate so dire
   As crowned his glory !

Flower of a noble, warlike race !
We greet you from this ancient place ,
God of your fathers grant you grace
   To fill your station :
May sons and daughters nobles grace
   In this great nation.

We're proud of Percy's honoured name,
So famed in ancient warlike theme ;

---

* The great Marquis of Argyle, beheaded 27th May 1685.—
" I could die like a Roman, but choose rather to die as a
Christian. I set the crown upon the King's head, but he gives
me a better crown than his own," said the great Argyle.

First in the fight their swords did gleam,
    And death's blows shower
But now their pennons peaceful stream
    From yon grey tower.

No longer from yon portal grey
A Percy rides to Border fray ;
No bleeding host at close of day
    Now enters there,
Behind whom dying comrades lay
    All spoiled and bare.

Long may their banners peaceful hing,
Their spears no more in battle ring,
But future bards their vict'ries sing
    In virtue's race.
And future lords their wisdom bring
    To bless this place.

God bless the two made one this day,
Sincere we men of Alnwick pray,
Be 't theirs to see their children grey,
    And great and wise ;
That crowds at *last* their dust may lay
    With tearful eyes.

MY OWN FIRESIDE.

There is a halo round the poor man's hearth
    Shines on his own fireside,
And cheers his weary downcast heart.
    That is oft sorely tried;
Through the toilsome day his thoughts will stray,
    And there with pleasure 'bide,
Cheered with the hope of joys to come
    Around his own fireside.

In that sacred spot, that heaven on earth,
    The poor man's own fireside,
May love and peace find there a place,
    In every heart preside.
Though coarse his fare, and daily toil
    Is still the poor man's lot,
Content and hope may crown his board,
    And sanctify the spot.

Perchance around his humble board
    A numerous offspring stand;
Though scanty clad and humbly fed,
    They're nourished by his hand.

The pious man, with thankful heart,
   Sends up a prayer on high,
For God to grant them daily bread,
   And guide them with His eye.

His little flock at evening-tide
   Meets round the fire to play,
And laugh together o'er the sports
   That pleased them through the day.
Oh! happy hours when the children sport
   Like kittens round the fire;
They're angels sent to bless the house,
   And draw our thoughts up higher.

  . But, cheerless homes, alas! there are
   In this dear land of ours:
No sunshine of the soul comes in
   To nurse life's tender flowers;
But clouds and darkness hover o'er
   Their fireless hearths and home,
That drive the half-clad children forth,
   With vice and sin to roam.

The starving mother, pinched and worn,
   Sits helpless with despair,
Her heart bleeds for the infant form
   That plays around her chair:

The father, guardian of their hearth,
  Is faithless to his trust,
In drunken revels spends his time
  In the vile haunts of lust.

LINES WRITTEN ON THE TOP OF BENRINNES,

DURING A VISIT TO STRATHSPEY IN AUGUST 1869.

Now here again I take my rest
Upon this mountain's rugged crest.
Although it's not by Nature dressed
   The heart to cheer,
There is no spot my foot has pressed
   To me more dear.

Far as I scan o'er hill and plain,
I mark each well-known spot again;
Then up comes Fancy with her train
   Of scenes long past—
Of clansmen rushing from each glen
   To pibroch's blast.

Instead of warlike mountaineer,
That sought the carnage with a cheer,
The frugal sons of toil appear
   In every place;
These smiling valleys far and near
   Are blessed with peace.

To eastward now I cast my eye,
And Moray's fertile plains descry,
With golden fields spread to the sky
   Fair to be seen,
Where fatt'ning herds recumbent lie
   On richest green.

And now I turn my feasted eyes
To where you see yon smoke arise ;
There Elgin's ancient city lies,
   Boast of the land ;
There busy man his commerce plies
   With ardent hand.

But tired with gazing on the plain,
I turn to dear Strathspey again ;
I mark the river join the main
   'Midst foam and spray ;
Backward I trace its course again
   To mountains grey.

Yonder, embowered in living green,
Proud Castle Gordon's towers are seen,
With many a verdant glade to screen
   Idlers that stray
'Neath spreading trees, love's favourite scene,
   At close of day.

My wandering eyes with pleasure rest
Upon Beneagen's pine-clad breast,
Where, sheltered like some cosy nest,
      A home appears
The poor and needy oft have blessed
      Amid their tears.

That graceful arch the river clears
Where Craigellachie's rock up-rears ;
All egress on that side appears
      Man's skill to mock ;
But yet his toil a highway clears
      Through solid rock.

I mark where stood M'Allan's shrine,
Where many a warrior's bones recline—
Brave warriors of that ancient line
      That stood war's shock,
Firm as the hardy mountain-pine
      That crowns the rock.

From this I turn to gaze upon
A mansion built of polished stone ;
And this fair spot doth virtue own
      With maiden grace,
With open hand her bounty sown
      Through all the place.

There Elchie's turrets meet the sky,
High o'er the woods that round them lie,—
Woods that a hermit might envie
        And find a place ;
But forms amongst them often stray
        Would mar his peace.

Where yon blue curling smoke doth rise,
Old Carron's ancient homestead lies ;
To it the traveller turns his eyes
        And feasts them there,
Where verdant fields spread to the skies
        Like garden fair.

A fairer spot is seldom seen,
Embowered 'mid trees of living green,
With many a ferny glade between
        And bosky dells ;
The home of Grant it long has been,
        As history tells.

Scenes meet my eyes on every hand,
The pride and glory of our land ;
Famed spots, whose names will ever stand
        In future story,
Firm as the giant hills around
        In all their glory.

Years have fast and silent fled
Since last along those vales I strayed,
And many a head is lowly laid
   That shared my joy,
There silent in the narrow bed,
   Nought to annoy.

With sobered thoughts I take my way
Where once I spent life's happy day;
A voice within me seems to say—
   All now is changed;
No more with comrades dear you'll stray
   Where oft you ranged:

For some have crossed the rolling deep,
To torrid climes where reptiles creep;
Untimely there they sleep death's sleep,
   Ne'er to return;
And for them childless mothers weep,
   And sadly mourn.

*LAMENT.

WRITTEN ON READING OF THE DEATH OF THE LATE EARL OF FIFE.

How can my muse now joyous sing !
How can she strike the vocal string ?
She sighing droops her dowie wing,
   Wi' grief opprest ;
Her fondest hopes did round him cling
   That's gane to rest.

Oh ! cruel Death ! thy fatal dart
Hath pierced his warm and feeling heart,
An' we aneath the stroke maun smart,
   An' sadly groan.
Wha noo will tak' the widow's part,
   Whan he is gone ?

Whaur noo will puir folks, in their need,
Tak' shelter frae th' oppressor's greed ?
They noo may bend them like a reed
   Their stay is gone ;
He was the poor man's friend indeed,
   They're left alone.

K

Nane frae his door he turned awa ;
He ne'er was deaf to sorrow's ca' ;
When cottars' backs were at the wa',
   He heard their tale,
An' took their part, baith ane an' a',
    An' wished them weel.

Feint ane cared less for pride an' state,
Nor sat mair lichtly on his seat ;
His smiling face was aye a treat
   To look upon ;
His feeling heart was truly great,
    But that is gone.

Nae social gatherins noo he'll grace,
Wi' kindly smile upon his face ;
But lone and empty is the place
   He graced wi' ease ;
Nae mair will joy licht up the face
    That aye could please.

Come, a' ye bards frae Ness to Dee,
Frae Cairngorum to the sea ;
Come join his cor'nach-wail wi' me—
   In chorus join ;
Pray that another like as he
    May fill his line.

Come, a' ye cottars, mourn the day
You saw him laid aneath the clay ;
Nae mair to him you'll tak' yer way,
   Wi' heavy heart ;
Nae mair, alas ! he'll be yer stay,
   Nor tak' yer part.

Let hireling bardies in their lays
The loudest sing to him that pays,
I scorn to follow in their ways—
   I only mourn
The noble man that lowly lies,
   Ne'er to return.

.

THE TRYSTING-TREE.

I KEN wha's waiting in the glen,
　　Beneath the trysting-tree ;
And, oh ! I ken his heart beats fast,
　　And a' for love o' me.
My blessing on yon bonnie star—
　　The star o' hope to me ;
It tells me that my Jamie waits
　　Beneath the trysting-tree.

I ken there's Nelly o' the bog
　　Would her broad acres gie,
If she could only get a glance
　　O' his soft pawky e'e.
Weel do I ken his heart's my ain,
　　Nane fairer does he see ;
And often has he told me this
　　Beneath the trysting-tree.

'Tis true he has nae acres broad,
　　Nor riches yet has he ;

But then he has a true, leal heart,
 An' that's mair dear to me.
I wadna gie a stowan glance
 Frae his saft, sparklin' e'e,
To be a queen, and change my place
 Beneath the trysting-tree.

Awa wi' wealth, awa wi' pelf—
 Can they mak' hearts agree ?
If for their sake we sell our love,
 Can there true pleasure be ?
Gie me the kind, the loving heart,
 That shines out through the e'e ;
And such a smile I've often seen
 Beneath the trysting-tree.

Now lordly dames may laugh at this,
 Nor think that love could be,
Or noble thoughts rise in a heart
 Wi' naething else tae gie.
It's nae the shining dust o' earth
 That mak's the man to me ;
But noble thoughts and burning words
 I've heard beneath yon tree.

But now the moon, wi' laughin' face,
 Peeps o'er Beneagan hie,

An' I'll down by the gowan bog,
 Where nane I'm sure can see ;
For weel I ken he anxious waits,
 Wi' keen and piercing e'e.
Oh ! speed the time we meet for aye
 Beneath our ain roof-tree.

TO MY ROBIN REDBREAST.

Now keenly blows the northern blast,
Like winter hail the leaves fall fast,
And my pet Robin's come at last
   To our old thorn ;
With warbling throat and eye upcast
   He greets the morn :

Like some true friend you come to cheer,
When all around is dark and drear,
And oh ! what friend to me more dear
   Than your sweet sel' ?
Your mellow voice falls on my ear
   Like some sweet spell.

Oft at the gloaming's pensive hour,
When clouds above me darkly lower,
I've sought a seat in some lone bower,
   With heart opprest ;
You soothed me with your magic power,
   And calmed my breast.

TO MY ROBIN REDBREAST.

When morning dons her sober grey
To usher in the coming day,
And Phœbus shines with sickly ray
      On all around,
No warblers greet him from the spray
      With joyous sound.

But you, sweet bird, unlike the throng,
Salute him with a joyous song.
When heavy rains and sleet prolong
      The dreary day,
You chant to him your evening song
      Upon the spray.

No blackbird whistles in the grove,
Where late in chorus sweet they strove;
No warbler's tongue is heard to move,
      But all is sad;
No cushat woos his amorous love
      In hazel glade.

TO THE SNOWDROP.

FAIREST and first of a glorious train !
I bid you welcome, sweet flower, again ;
For you come the first of the floral band
We shall soon see spread over all the land.
Though no vernal sun, with life-giving ray,
Bids you welcome on this wintery day,
You come like angel with message of love—
A pledge of remembrance from heaven above.

Sweet little flower ! as you spring by my door,
You teach me a lesson unheeded before,
Of Him who ordained thee to spring and blow
Amid keen biting winds and sleety snow ;
Fit emblem thou of that mystery deep,
When man will rise from death's long sleep ;
From the womb of earth he'll spring like a flower
To be gathered by God for His heavenly bower.

Sweet little flower ! as you spring by my door,
You bid me hope on 'mid my scanty store,

And bravely trust, amid the cares and strife,
And the weary toil of this up-hill life.
In the dark cheerless morn I pass you by,
Toiling and growing 'neath a sunless sky,
And I've thought, perchance, e'er the dark day close,
You may find a grave 'neath the wint'ry snows.

Sweet little flower ! as you spring by my door,
You teach me more than e'er I knew before
Of the heartfelt pleasure a flower can give,
For it is not in vain you bloom and live.
But thoughtless man, on earthly pleasure bent,
No wisdom sees in the flowers that are sent ;
A heavenly mentor, by his path you stand,
And bid him pause and think of the better land.

Sweet little flower ! as you spring by my door,
I love you more than I e'er did before,
For the very same Hand that made you a flower,
Made heaven and earth by the word of His power,
And gave to my spirit a feeling of love,
A longing desire for the garden above ;
For the flowers never fade in that glorious land,
Like Him who has made them, immortal they stand.

"THERE'S A PRETTY WEE HOUSIE PROVIDIN' FOR ME."

DEDICATED TO THE MORAY LASSES.

THERE'S a pretty wee housie providin' for me,
And in it, I trow, we shall soon happy be ;
There isna the like o't, I'm sure, in the glen,
Wi' sae canty a *but*, an' sae coothie a *ben*.
It's true we'll hae naething sae grand or sae braw,
As the great folks wha live in a castle or ha' ;
But I am sure we'll hae plenty, if only content,
And thankfu' to Him who our blessings has sent.

I ken we'll be happy :—our housie will be
A little bit heaven to Jamie and me ;
When cares shall oppress him, and sadden his face,
To soothe and divert him I ken it's my place ;
And when he comes hame frae his day's weary toil,
I'll hae a clean hearth, and a sweet winning smile ;
There's naething, I'm sure, he likes better to see,
Than a clean cosy hearth, and a smile upon me.

And when winter winds blaw wi' snell biting breath,
And Nature aroun' us is frozen in death,
We'll shut oot the day, wi' its glimmer o' licht,
And never complain o' a lang, weary nicht.
Whiles Jamie 'll read, or I'll lilt a bit sang,
And wi' cracking and joking we'll nae think it lang;
And aye the last thing ere we gang to our rest,
We will seek His direction wha kens to guide best.

When summer comes roun' wi' its sweet sunny hours,
And breezes come laden wi' scent o' the flowers,
We'll stray by the burnie where scented birks hing,
And listen how sweetly the birdies can sing.
Far, far frae the bustle and turmoil o' life,
We'll jog on life's journey and never ken strife;
Wi' griefs we may meet that are ill to be borne,
To-day may seem dark, but we'll hope a bright morn.

We a' ken that riches can never buy health,
And a wise man has said that contentment is wealth;
And if we have these, we'll be richer by far,
Than "my lord" who struts gaily wi' ribbon and star.
But contentment and riches may often be found,
Like a fruit-bearing tree, showering blessings around;
And happy the spot where their branches are spread,
And happy the people that dwell in their shade.

A CHRISTMAS GREETING

TO MY KIND FRIEND, ANTHONY OLIVER GARDENER, ESLINGTON PARK.

A MERRY Christmas, friend, I wish you !
May heaven with its blessings bless you !
Be 't many a year before we miss you
   From that sweet spot
Where Providence has kindly placed you,
   And cast your lot.

Yule is a time to cheer the heart,
For friends to meet that are apart ;
The rich to heal the biting smart
   Of care and want,
For little cheers the drooping heart
   When bread is scant.

Oh ! that the rich folks only knew
What good a little wealth can do !
Alas ! I fear they are but few
   That think of this ;
But then they lose the heavenly dew,
   The poor man's bliss.

I fear there's many a cupboard bare,
With neither bread nor Christmas fare,
While misery and dark despair
       Brood o'er the place;
The smallest thing that we can spare
       Would help their case.

All that we have, it's God that sent it,
It's not our own, He's only lent it;
For to do good we know He meant it,
       To all around;
If foolishly we run and spend it,
       We're faithless found.

A gift this day from heaven was sent—
God gave it us, it was not lent.
When angels o'er the manger bent
       They sang this song—
" Lo ! now the Father's gift is sent,
       The promised long."

This gift can cheer the humble cot,
Can sanctify the poor man's lot,
And consecrate the humblest spot
       In all the land;
Brings honour to the russet coat
       And horny hand.

This gift is offered free to all,
To rich and poor, to great and small :
Men worldly treasures riches call ;
        But let them try,
They'll find their value is but small
        This gift to buy.

What is this gift, of which we boast,
That men may have so free from cost ?
It is the innocence we lost
        That mournful day
When men the fatal bound'ry crossed
        Where evil lay.

Life's ills now cloud earth's fairest spot,
And come alike to hall and cot ;
Those ills *we make*, I'll name them not,
        Make thousands weep,
And sore bewail their bitter lot
        In sorrow deep.

These ills make sad hearts long to rise,
And leave this earth, where sorrow tries,
For sinless world beyond the skies
        They long to go ;
But when man to heaven would rise,
        He aims too low.

And many a suffering soul's opprest,
A thousand sorrows rend their breast ;
The grave alone can give that rest
    They seek in vain ;
Let's strive to get their wrongs redrest,
    And save them pain.

Alas ! in this loved land of ours,
Where freedom's sun his radiance pours,
The thorns spring up amidst the flowers,
    And take their room,
And rob them of sweet vernal showers,
    And spoil their bloom.

When we our happy Christmas keep,
Let's not forget that others weep,
For when we're calm in peaceful sleep,
    There are I fear
Who'll groan in anguish far too deep
    For sigh or tear.

But let us work, my friend, and pray
For strength and patience for our day,
And friends our old grey heads to lay
    In their last rest ;
May all that knew us kindly say,
    " They did their best."

THE TOOM MEAL-KIST.

SUGGESTED BY READING AN EDITOR'S ARTICLE IN THE
"ELGIN COURANT," ENTITLED "RELIEF TO THE
POOR."

> " 'Mang herds and honest country folk,
>   That till the farm and feed the flock,
>   Careless o' mair ; wha never fash
>   To lade their kist wi' useless cash ;
>   But thank the gods for what they've sent
>   O' health eneugh and blithe content,
>   And pith that helps them to stravaig
>   Ower ilka cleugh and ilka craig."
>   —FERGUSSON.

YE that are happit snug and warm,
  In these cauld winter days,
Ye canna feel the poor man's griefs,
  His sorrows and his waes.
While ye sit roun' your cosy fires,
  Wi' a' your comforts blest,
He sits beside his cheerless hearth
  And eyes that toom meal-kist.

* Toom, empty; meal-kist it was a common practice in
Scotland to keep a store of meal in a kist or girnel.

L

Beside him sits his patient wife,
　　The partner o' his waes,
And wi' a mither's skill she mends
　　The bairnies' raggit claes ;
Then, wi' a noble woman's heart,
　　She bids him hope and trust,
That brighter days will soon be here,
　　To fill the toom meal-kist.

But while the words o' comfort flow
　　That cheer the downcast man,
A silent, unseen tear drops soft
　　Upon her wasted han'.
Oh ! who can tell what sorrows wring
　　A mother's loving breast,
While round her sleep those helpless things
　　Beside a toom meal-kist ?

Ye thoughtless throng, ye giddy fair,
　　That mad with folly flirt,
And try how many yards to wear,
　　In one enormous skirt ;
Like silly peacock, vain and proud,
　　Dear self fills all your breast ;
Look at that half-clad woman there
　　With but a toom meal-kist !

Ye rich guidwives, whose stores o'erflow
  In larder and in press,
Oh! think that He who blessed you so
  Can quickly make them less.
If we a sister see in need,
  And hard wi' want opprest,
A heavenly blessing will be ours,
  To fill her toom meal-kist.

And you, rich, vain, proud man, who think
  That you are Heaven's care,
Because He has filled your barns full
  And left your neighbour's bare.
The poor in spirit, rich in faith,
  By Heaven alone are blest,
And the poor man may be rich in full,
  With but a toom meal-kist.

And you, ye mad and thoughtless throng,
  That nightly round the bowl
Spend what would buy the orphans food
  And cheer the widow's soul;
But think how small the poor man's need,
  And what ye thoughtless waste;
'Twould bring a blessing on your head,
  To fill his toom meal-kist.

ON THE DEATH OF THE YEAR 1855.

DEDICATED TO SAUNDERS M'GREGOR.

STEEK fast the door, an' dinna jingle;
Draw ben your chair beside the ingle;
Now tak' a glass to cheer your heart,
The best o' friens, alas! maun pairt.
O Tibby, Tibby! mak' less din,
Ye ken yersel' wha's sick within.
Puir Fifty-Five has ta'en his bed,
And ne'er again the grass will tread.
The Doctor says at twal' o'clock
He's sure to hae a mortal shock.
But hark! he raps upon the hallan,
He cries, "Guidman, bring in the callan'!
Bring Fifty-Sax, for I must go
To dark oblivion's shades below.
And now, my son, just gie's your hand,
Ye ken I soon maun leave this land;
And when I'm dead an' maist forgot,
There's some will try my name to blot.

I muckle doubt they'll sair misca' me ;
Aye, e'en to folk wha never saw me.
They'll say I spent their cash for nought,
And dear they paid for a' they bought.
They'll say I made their pantries toom,
And kept a better frae my room.
A' this ye'll hear, an' muckle mair ;
I ken my name they winna spare.
Let this, my son, ne'er grieve your heart,
But nobly act a manly pairt.
O Fifty-Sax ! propitious smile
On that dear spot called Britain's isle !
And open wide auld Nature's hand,
And scatter plenty o'er their land.
Oh ! send them peace wi' honour crowned,
And gird them safe wi' virtues round ;
And then, my son, I winna fear,
Ye'll nobly fill your daddy's chair ! "

LINES INSCRIBED TO SAUNDERS M'GREGOR,

A MEMBER OF THE ROUND-TABLE CLUB, ELGIN, JULY 1857.

HERE am I choked wi' dust and reek,
For rest and quiet I vainly seek,
Nought but the everlasting squeak
   Of rattling engines,
You scarce can hear a neighbour speak
   For their loud vengeance.

Here night and day our sky's o'ercast
Wi' choking reek from Mammon's blast,
So thick, that had a comet passed,
   We wadna kent it,
But lived in ignorance to the last
   That God had sent it.

O Saunders, man! were ye but here,
To see the bustling noise and steer!
Folks hardly can find time to speer
   For friend or foe;
A wink or nod, and past you clear,
   And on they go.

Weel may ye crack o' broomy knowes,
Where yet in peace the wild deer browse ;
There's not on earth such heights and howes
      As ye possess,
And bonny glens where cowslip grows
      In golden dress.

You note each day the growing crap,
And rest yourself in Nature's lap,
And when inclined, you toddlin' stap
      By glen or burn,
Where scented dews frae birch-trees drap
      At every turn.

You little ken what ye possess ;
Wi' blessings rife, you prize them less :
You've Nature decked in flowery dress
      Your eyes to please,
And kind old friends your hand to press
      And heart to ease.

But, ah ! my friend, it's sad to think
How men the chains o' folly clink,
And oft prefer some stagnant sink
      To Nature's rill ;
At her sweet stream men seldom drink
      And take their fill.

Oft when I read your social crack,
On memory's wings my fancy's back
To simple joys, that ne'er did lack
   A pleasure true :
But now men's brains are on the rack
   For something new.

Pure simple pleasure gives a joy
Which softens cares that oft annoy ;
And never leaves that base alloy
   O' future grief,
That does man's happiness destroy
   Wi' no relief.

Forced by necessity's grim will,
Thousands sweat in forge and mill ;
They seldom taste of Nature's rill :
   O' dust and reek
Day after day they drink their fill,
   Till pale the cheek.

And, sad to think, there's many seek
Their pleasure in what makes men weak :
In filthy dens, where poisons reek,
   Their evenings spend,—-
A poor solace for toil-spent week—
   When thus it ends.

Their home is not that sacred place,
The pure abode of joy and peace ;
And there we see the haggard face
       O' want and sin,
And misery we plainly trace
       On a' within.

We boast o' being rich and great,
A prosp'rous and a glorious state,
And that each man his bread may eat
       Beneath his tree ;
But luxury may sap a state,
       Though great it be.

If with a retrospective eye
We view the years so long gone by,
A warning from them seems to cry,
       With outraged patience,
That there's a Power which rules on high,
       O'er men and nations.

LEEDS, *July* 1857.

MY LITTLE ROSEBUD.

My little rosebud, sweet and fair—
　　None fairer could be seen—
Bloomed sweetly 'neath my cottage eaves,
　　Amidst its leaves so green.

And all that passed my cottage door
　　Admired my lovely rose ;
They said it rivalled every flower
　　That in the garden grows.

With tender care I nursed my flower,
　　I joyed to see it grow,
And spread its petals to the sun,
　　Pure as the driven snow.

Safe from the sun's fierce burning rays,
　　I shielded it with care,
And when the evening dew fell soft,
　　Its fragrance filled the air.

Oft by its side I loved to sit,
　　When the day's toil was done,

Wondering what made sweet flowers grow,
  While glorious sank the sun.

Then heavy thoughts stole o'er my heart,
  I knew my flower must die,
And, like all earthly-born things,
  Must wither and decay.

My boding fears, alas! proved true,
  For soon my lovely flower
Fell soiled and scattered on the earth,
  Beneath a midnight shower.

I gathered up the fallen leaves,
  That once were sweet and fair,
And in a drawer I them did lay,
  With tender loving care.

When winter comes with sunless sky,
  With darkness and with gloom,
My fallen rose of the summer,
  With fragrance fills my room.

My rose to me a lesson taught,
  That beauty, when alone,
Will never any fragrance yield,
  When its fair colour's gone.

A CHRISTMAS SONG.

We hail again the natal morn
On which the Prince of Peace was born—
Born to draw us sinful men
Back to our Father's love again.
Again we raise the heavenly strain
Of "Peace on earth, good-will to men;"
God's choicest gift to man is given,
His own belovèd Son from heaven.

But "Him we will not have to reign,"
Is still the universal strain;
And gentle Peace, with tearful eye,
Weeps where the slain in thousands lie.
Yes! at a despot's high command,
Men raise the fratricidal hand;
We, shuddering, turn our straining eyes
To where the groans of battle rise,

And wonder when this strife shall cease,
And nations long and pray for peace—

When shall come that glorious time,
When peace shall reign in every clime,
And men, like brothers, hand in hand,
Join in the sweet fraternal band
That owns that Prince's peaceful sway
Whose birth we celebrate to-day.

Let us the holly bring and bay
To deck our homes this festal day,
And stir the yule-log to a blaze,
While thankful we our songs do raise
To Him our Heavenly King above,
Who came this day in peace and love.
And soon may He descend again,
Upon this troubled earth to reign !

A SECOND EPISTLE TO SAUNDERS M'GREGOR.

How pleasant is the summer day,
With dewy dawn and evening grey !
Then books and papers past we lay
      With right good will,
And with a crony saunt'ring stray
      Through glen or hill.

To me the *Times* has now no charms,
'Tis filled with nought but war's alarms,
Of mighty feats by men in arms,
      That kill and slay,
Just as the bees they kill in swarms
      On autumn day.

But I will say 't, and think no shame,
That I abhor a warlike theme,
All strife where swords and sulphur gleam,
      And bullets fly ;
War I prefer where, killed or lame,
      None writhing lie.

The war of wives, with head-gear torn,
I need not say that has my scorn,
Though hero-like they're sometimes borne
                    From off the field,
While of their locks perhaps they're shorn,
                    And bruised and peeled.

Domestic war, we know, is rife—
The war of words, without the knife ;
I mean, the war 'tween man and wife
                    Is sometimes bloody ;
It seldom ends but with the life
                    Of either body.

But let us turn to that famed field,
Where statesmen keen their weapons wield.
How deftly they can fence and shield,
                    And cut and thrust!
Beneath their blows the brave have reeled,
                    And bit the dust.

Two mighty champions take the field,
And well their weapons both can wield ;
One takes the broadsword and the shield,
                    And lays about him ;
The deadly spear the other wields,
                    And tries to rout him.

Each is the leader of a band,
Ready to do their chief's command,
And for his cause they'll boldly stand,
                    Be 't right or wrong ;
" Our people's rights and native land,"
                    Is their old song.

One champion in the end must fall,
The weakest soon goes to the wall ;
Then their war trumpet's clam'rous call
                    Sounds through the nation,
All to revenge their champion's fall,
                    From his high station.

Men fight another warfare still—
Instead of blood, 'tis ink they spill,
And with the pen they try to kill
                    Their deadly foe ;
Till of revenge they drink their fill,
                    And lay him low.

TO MY AULD PIKE STAFF.

My auld pike staff, my trusty frien',
Like hand and glove we aye hae been;
Mony a change we baith hae seen,
   Since first we met;
Atween us yet nae words hae been,
    I'm prood to say't.

Well do I mind the April morn
I took you frae your parent thorn.
Although at times you've been the scorn
   O' modern pride,
I ne'er could bide to hae you shorn
   O' bark or hide.

A varnished coat ye ne'er could shaw,
Like sticks that come frae far awa;
Nor were you ever busket braw
    Wi' dangling tassel;
But aye a sturdy shank could shaw,
    To bide a brassel.

M

When I to kirk or market gaed,
You aye did help me in my need;
I didna want a hicc'ry reed
            Like strutting spark;
They look nae better than a weed,
               And dae nae wark.

Ower hills and glens I've wandered wide
With you aye faithful by my side;
Down craigs and rocks you've been my guide,
            And kept me right;
With you I ne'er felt dashed nor fleyed
             In darkest night.

On many a wild-goose chase we've been,
When I was thoughtless, young, and green;
Full forty miles we've often gane
            On summer's day,
When some famed spot was to be seen,
             Where heroes lay.

But now auld age is come at last,
And all those thoughtless days are past,
And oh, alas! they vanished fast,
            Like some sweet dream;
For them I'll raise nae mournful blast,
             Nae poet's theme.

TO MY AULD PIKE STAFF.

We count our years now by the score,
Our furthest journey 's round the door ;
New scenes we'll ne'er again explore,
    'Mid Nature's charms ;
But thought of what we've seen before
    My old heart warms.

They thoughtless folks may sneer and laugh
At you and me, my auld pike staff ;
We'll little heed their idle chaff,
    But toddle on ;
You'll be my friend, my auld pike staff,
    Till I am gone.

AN ODE WRITTEN ON THE CENTENARY
OF SIR WALTER SCOTT.

Scotland resigns this day to Scott,
    And hails this morn—
The day she never shall forget,
    When he was born.
He, like some glorious comet bright,
    Has crossed our sky;
His radiance dimmed the stars of night
    That round him lie.

His glory is no meteor-light,
    But, like the sun,
He'll shine with undiminished rays
    Till time is done,
Till ocean old shall cease to roll
    And rivers flow;
Till then our Wizard's name shall live
    With men below.

No higher fame can mortals know,
    Where life is death,
And human glory here below
    Is but a breath ;
But there's a soul that lives in man
    Knows no decay :
It has a voice when he is gone,
    And passed away.

Scott, like some prophet-seer of old,
    Whose soul had been
To that ethereal spirit-world
    Unseen by men,
Had early learned that mystic art,
    To cast a spell
Of glamour o'er the human heart,
    That men love well.

For at his word men live again,
    And feast our eyes :
He waves his pen, and angel forms
    Drop from the skies :
We see them walk this earth again,
    And hear them speak ;
Entranced we gaze with beating heart
    And glowing cheek.

And o'er the mighty dead of old
    He cast his spell,
And made them to our list'ning ears
    Their story tell,
Of ancient feud and bloody strife,
    Of hate and love,
And all the varied passions deep,
    That hearts can move.

POOR DOEY IS DEAD: A LAMENT.

Poor Doey's dead, and rests her head
    Beneath a moss-grown tree;
We placed her there with tears and care,—
    I mean, my wife and me;
We neither spoke, nor silence broke,
    But in our hearts we said,
"Our old friend's gone, and we're alone.
    Our poor dog's lowly laid."

She was ill bred, the dog-folk said;
    But her heart was kind, I know.
If her tail was thick, and like a stick,
    She had only part to show.
In circles round I've seen her bound
    For half a summer's day,
And try by might, by wrong and right,
    The stump to tear away.

She'll lie no more beside the door,
    To watch when I come home,

And say, as plain as dog could say,
　　"Let's down the green lane roam."
Poor Doey's laid, as I have said,
　　Beneath a spreading tree ;
No more she'll run, when day is done,
　　Along the lanes with me.

AN EPISTLE TO MR. J. THOMSON.

AND so, my friend, you mean to taste
　　An author's toil and care,
Hoping that smiling Fame may have
　　A laurel leaf to spare,
A fresh green leaf without a stain,
To show you have not sung in vain.

I wish you in the task success
　　Which you have undertaken,
And trust that by no cross unseen,
　　Your purpose may be shaken ;
For difficulties oft arise,
When we seem nearest to the prize.

The lyre the master-minstrel sweeps,
　　With bowèd heads men pause to hear ;
And though its thrilling music clothe
　　A worthless theme, he needs not fear :
The distant zenith holds his star,
Its rays to beauty turn each scar.

But when some nameless minstrel strikes
  His trembling lyre with blush and stammer,
His measure, rhythm, rhyme are scanned,
  And woe betide his hapless grammar.
What wonder if he shrink and shiver,
And turn his back on fame for ever!

More to the poet's heart than fame,
  As life and freedom dear,
Is Nature, quiet or wildly grand.
  Howe'er she may appear.
To him the stream, the daisied sod,
Have each a voice which speaks of God.

When sorrow o'er his chequered path
  Its sombre mantle flings,
Should foes triumph, or friends forsake,
  Amid the clouds he sings:
His grandest or his sweetest strain
Is born of wrong or wrung by pain.

Not from the gory battle-field
  Does inspiration come,
Not from the flashing steel, nor speaks
  It in the rolling drum.
The poet gazes on afar,
And sees but Glory's gilded car.

Glory !—alas ! that e'er its praise
    The poet should have sung,
That e'er earth's hills and dales should have
    With martial music rung,
The voice of human love to smother,
And urge men to destroy each other !

Be 't ours to hail a better day,
    When Glory's dazzling glare
Shall blind no more, nor blight the earth
    With ruin and despair.
Be 't ours to sing of peace and love,
Which, blessing earth, is crowned above.

The world is wide, and sunlight free,
    And free the balmy air ;
Some close their hearts 'gainst warmth and light,
    Some catch a double share ;
And while for all the sun is shining,
The half are 'mid the clouds repining.

If on thy heart a double share
    Of warmth and radiance streams,
Give back to those who see them not
    Some pure life-giving beams,
Mellowed and softened by the touch
Of love, which bears and pardons much.

There may be hearts thy song will reach,
   And rouse to courage, soothe to peace ;
It may touch chords whose echoing tones
   Not ev'n with life itself shall cease.
Then why should'st thou in secret sing,
Though no proud wreath thy song may bring ?

There's blood upon the conqueror's bays,
   Tears dim the patriot's crown ;
Thorns bristle on the envied wreath
   The poet calls his own ;
And some perchance that wreath have worn
Who'd bruise the leaf to break the thorn.

Then forward with thy work, nor shrink
   From critic's blame or praise.
If here and there a heart may be
   Made better by thy lays,
Remember that is more than fame,
Than warrior's wreath or victor's name.

And now, farewell.   I ne'er before
   In rhyme a letter wrote,
And much I fear 'tis little worth ;
   But whether prized or not,
Your success will give joy to me,
And I remain, your friend, E. D.

AN ANSWER TO E. D.'S EPISTLE.

THANKS, Madam, for your letter kind,
It helped to soothe an anxious mind.
You, that have felt "an author's care,"
Know well the thought that's upmost there.
There Hope and Fear alternate reign,
I fight against them but in vain.
Fear says, "Beware, and hold your hand
Before you self-committed stand
A fool before 'the gods and men,'
Convicted by your own goose-pen."
Then Hope breathes whisper in my ear,
"Take heart of grace, and never fear;
If laurel wreath is not for thee,
Your head with daisies crowned shall be.
Though Fame for you no trumpet blow,
Love's oil upon your head shall flow."
And what is Fame compared to Love?
It is the theme of saints above.
Fame, Hope, and Fear, as all men know,
Beyond the grave can never go.

The Man of Sorrows came to show
The power of Love on earth below;
And when Love guides the poet's pen,
He's like an angel sent to men.
Who would not wish, in his last hour,
To leave behind a spirit-dower,
A voice to soothe the tempest-driven,
Like that the prophet heard from heaven?
This still small voice is calling still,
The same that spoke on Horeb's hill.
We hear it in the murm'ring breeze,
That stirs at eve the leafy trees;
We hear it in the rippling rill,
That dances down the ferny hill;
We hear it in the rustling corn,
When by the reapers it is shorn.
All Nature speaks in accents clear,
But man is deaf and will not hear;
By passion some are heedless driven,
They laugh at hell and jest at heaven;
They think them both a pious fraud,
To please the good and fright the bad.
If men's *belief* be false or true,
In this free land we've nought to do;
So long as they obey man's laws,
The state against them has no *cause*.
But there's a higher law of Love,
Vouchsafed to man from God above:

This law takes knowledge of the heart,
And bids us from all ill depart;
To others we must act and do
Like friends and brothers stanch and true:
Ourselves we must no longer please,
But cast behind us selfish ease.
Thus we must do if we desire
To hear that voice, " Friend, come up higher."
My friend! we see but dimly here,
Our eyes cannot see heaven clear,
But, like a "vision of the night,"
It seems to pass before our sight;
Like Job, in some lone midnight hour,
We tremble 'neath an unseen Power,
Then know we that there is on high,
A God with an all-seeing eye!